The Red Sox and the Devil's Handmaiden

A Tale of Magical Realism

Andy Plotkin

PublishAmerica
Baltimore

© 2005 by Andy Plotkin.
All rights reserved. No part of this book may be reproduced, stored in a retrieval system or transmitted in any form or by any means without the prior written permission of the publishers, except by a reviewer who may quote brief passages in a review to be printed in a newspaper, magazine or journal.

First printing

ISBN: 1-4137-8799-1 (softcover)
ISBN: 978-1-4489-7296-8 (hardcover)
PUBLISHED BY PUBLISHAMERICA, LLLP
www.publishamerica.com
Baltimore

Printed in the United States of America

Table of Contents

Dedication 5

Forward 7

A Note About the Historical Content 11

Introductory Note 13

The Red Sox and the Devil's Handmaiden 15

Dedication

I wish to dedicate this work to various people from whom I have learned creative approaches, technical skills, problem-solving abilities, and tenacity. To my mother, the famous artist Edna Hibel, I have learned a process of creativity and an approach to solving artistic problems. To my father, Tod Plotkin, I have learned the art of writing; specifically, that all prose is at heart poetic in nature.

From these three professors, the late Albert J. Sullivan, Professor Emeritus Bernard S. Phillips, and my late father-in-law, Bernard Rabin, I have learned that even the most erudite writing must strive for elegance and simplicity.

I would also like to express my gratitude to Millie Brown Clarkson, accomplished author, who has mentored me in writing. She encouraged me to write this story and to submit it to esteemed publishing houses, PublishAmerica foremost among them.

Finally, from my wife, Cheryll R. Plotkin, I have received more encouragement and love than any person deserves. I have also received much moral support from my children, Wendy R. Plotkin and Joshua R. Plotkin.

To all of these important people I owe more than I can say. To the readers who enjoy any part of this story, please take a moment to thank them. For any shortcomings you see, please know that they are mine alone.

Foreword

I wrote this story to try to come to grips with the fascinating genre of magical realism. In order to more fully enjoy this tall tale, I suggest that together we briefly explore what magical realism contains, and what it does not.

Events or happenstance that most people believe could occur according to the laws of physics or according to socially accepted norms of behavior are often defined as natural or "real." In apposition, anything that occurs in the realm of the supernatural, whether springing from Heaven or Hell, or even on Earth, may be referred to by a majority of people as "magical." "Magical realism" may therefore be defined as a story in which any event or happenstance occurs as a result of these two "realms"—the real and the magical—intermingling and affecting each other.

For example, an oral or written story that takes place solely in a supernatural location such as Heaven, perhaps only involving angels, cherubs, seraphims, and God, without reference to people or common objects, is magical—as well as religious—but not real. Oppositely, a tale set in the natural realm of people and common objects, without reference to gods or demons, is real, but not magical. However, if the protagonist in a story appeals to a Heavenly or other supernatural realm in order to affect some event on Earth, such as a protagonist's prayer for his mother to recover from a life-threatening illness, then this story can be defined as being within the genre of magical realism.

The line between realism and magic, however, is often blurred because typical occurrences on Earth, while known by a vast majority of people as being real, are nevertheless also frequently viewed as "miraculous" and "magical" by this same vast majority. A child's first smile, first step, and first word are often viewed in this magical way. Similarly, a full-arching rainbow is often seen like this.

Additionally, even when people believe that God is no longer an important influence during the Christmas season, they still often view people's good deeds in the name of Christmas and God as being miraculous. Feeding the hungry and homeless and giving clothes to the poor may be viewed as belonging to this miraculous category.

In sum, stories in which the realms of the real and the supernatural impact each other, and stories in which readers believe that the unfolding and resolution of events are in some way miraculous, are defined, in my opinion, as magical realism.

Looked at as a continuum, magically real stories can range from the most fantastical and bizarre to the most pedantic and mundane; from the most supernatural to the most natural; from the most sacred to the most profane; from the most metaphysical to the most physical; from the most magical to the most real. In the language of the physical world—the realm of science and technology—the genre of magical realism can range in stories from the least to the most probable; that is, from the least to the most believable.

The Red Sox and the Devil's Handmaiden, while referring often to every day—even earthy—events, falls on the far end of the supernatural scale. I mean, how probable is it for God and the Devil to appear before the same person at the same time? Frankly, I think not very likely, but please feel free to differ. Still, this and many other such fictions are written to show that magical elements can be manifested in even the most realistic of stories. By extension, I hope the readers' own lives are enriched, as mine has been from penning this tale.

Of course, you and I will disagree as to what extent the probability is of a specific event occurring in any story. Yet, I believe that what is most probable in all magical realism tales is that they juxtapose our normal world against a backdrop of unreality, and thereby throw reality into sharper relief. Such stories, if nothing else, help us to see greater beauty and other wondrous characteristics that we otherwise might overlook and take for granted. The coastal hills of California? Beautiful. These same hills set against the Pacific Ocean? Otherworldly. Unimaginable. Unbelievable. Miraculous. Magical.

Magical realism, even for those who categorically deny the existence of the supernatural, can extend all our senses, illuminate added emotional and intellectual dimensions, and help us appreciate our most realistic of worlds. The writing of the "Red Sox" story has been a magical odyssey for me. I hope it provides a similar journey for you.

A Note About the Historical Content

Taking advantage of the fact that one of the central characters of this story has witnessed over 5,600 years of history, I have woven various educational and philosophical concepts throughout the book. Some of these concepts concern the following: 1) how the religion of Judaism was advanced by various women in the Bible, including references to the lives of Sarah, Rebecca, Rachel, Leah, Dina, Tamar, Hannah, Miriam, and Esther; 2) the depiction of the Shechinah in a variety of Renaissance and Catholic art; 3) the roles of lust and love in a sacred relationship; 4) matriarchy and patriarchy, and the civil rights of women in Jewish and early Christian societies; 5) various concepts as they relate to their roles in modern and ancient societies, including prayer, justice, love, sex, mass media, terrorism, and chaos theory; and, as the proverbial advertising expression goes, 6) lots more!

Introductory Note

After the Boston Red Sox defeated the New York Yankees in a dramatic American League Playoff Series in October 2004, I was inspired to write a story against the backdrop of the Boston Red Sox's forthcoming World Series victory. Unbelievably, I completed the story prior to the Red Sox's final championship game—a foreshadowing of the miracles imagined in the story itself.

The Red Sox and the Devil's Handmaiden

Steve never grew tired of hearing the crack of the bat on the ball. Or the smack of the pitch in the catcher's mitt. Or the strident call of "steeriiike!" from the home plate umpire. *A little less smell of stale beer and junk food spilled all over the stands might be nice,* Steve thought, but hey, the emerald grass and the sight of the Green Monster, the most unusual outfield wall in all of baseball, were exciting as ever to him. He was inside Beantown's famous Yawkey's yard, Fenway Park, home of the Boston Red Sox.

Today, the sunlit azure blue sky, punctuated with puffy cumulus clouds, crackled with new autumn air. Part of Steve thought he was in heaven, because at age thirty-five he was finally able to obtain season tickets behind home plate. Another part of him knew he was in Hell, because due to the Curse of the Bambino, his beloved—and exasperating—Red Sox seemed doomed never to win another World Series—the last such victory being eighty-six years ago.

This particular game was one of the last in the 2004 season. It was a meaningless game in terms of the team's standing within the American League. The Sox had made a valiant effort to close the gap with their perennial New York Yankee nemesis, but they couldn't overtake them now. And yet, the Red Sox had secured a berth in the Playoffs as the wild card, the second-place team with the best record among the three second-place teams in their respective divisions within their league. In fact, the Red Sox record this year was so good, Steve knew, that the team had more victories than both of the first place teams in the other divisions. Only the dratted Yankees had a superior record in the league, giving them a home field advantage in the Playoffs. Gnashing his teeth, Steve chafed at this thought.

During the long season, Steve had become friendly with Nancy, the lady in the seat to his left. She had a pleasant, and generally quiet disposition, and cheered with restraint at the appropriate moments. Throughout this game, though, Nancy was unusually boisterous, standing and sitting, whooping it up, waving her arms, clapping her hands, and just giggling and beaming ebullient smiles. He hadn't recalled such enthusiasm from her when the games were really important, and now…now that it didn't matter, she seemed overly ecstatic for his taste.

"Are you drunk?" Steve jovially asked Nancy between innings. He didn't see how she could be, because he hadn't seen her drinking any beer.

"Who me?" She smiled. "No, I don't think so, unless they spiked the soda I just drank," she quipped. "And what if I *am* drunk?"

"I-I didn't mean anything by it." He paused, embarrassed. "I guess I can't figure out why you'd be so...so spirited when the game doesn't mean that much for the Playoffs."

"Huh," she snorted, "and here I thought you were a connoisseur of the game of baseball." He was taken aback, but allowed her to continue without comment. "There are a couple of reasons this game matters. First of all, you'll notice that several of the starters are sitting out the game, resting up for the Playoffs. So I'm cheering on their substitutes. Notice also that the normal pitching order has been changed so that the starting rotation will be what the manager wants at the beginning of the Playoffs."

"Oh, that's right. Of course, but, I didn't know—"

"Yeah, yeah, I'm a woman, so what—"

"Hold it," he interjected. "I'm not prejudiced against women. Certainly women can be experts at the game. Heck, without women, professional baseball might have died out in the thirties and forties. It was radio—and a few savvy team owners—who first lured women into the stands and allowed both leagues to survive."

Impressed, she asked, "How did you know that?"

"I'm a connoisseur, as you say," he beamed with smug satisfaction. "What's your other reason for being so, uh, full of verve?"

"I guess I'm just giddy, because I've been told this is the year."

"The year?" Steve asked with a puzzled look.

"Yes, of course. The year for the Red Sox to win the World Series."

"You were told? By whom? And do you actually *believe* this person?" he challenged.

"Look," Nancy replied, "I'm hungry. So let's watch the end of the game, and then you can take me to eat at Durgin Park, and I'll tell you everything. Okay?"

"Did…did you just ask yourself out on a date with me?"

Turning red, she covered up her mouth while she giggled. "Yeah, I guess I did, didn't I? I'm sorry. Do you mind?"

"N-No," he shook his head bewildered, wondering what the heck just happened. "I guess it's so…so two thousandish," he laughed. He extended his hand now in jest. "Hi, I'm Steve, and I'm taking you to Durgin Park after the game…whether I like it or not."

She chuckled and responded by shaking his hand. "And I'm Nancy. Thanks for making me ask you out." They both enjoyed a hearty laugh and then turned their faces to the play on the field.

While she was engrossed in the game, he surreptitiously scrutinized her and tried to sort out what was happening. He didn't recall Nancy ever jumping and waving her arms during prior games. In fact, he didn't recall losing his breath before at the sight of her bobbing breasts straining magnificently against her bra and shirt.

Was she always that large? he thought. *In fact, look at those shapely legs. All through the hot summer she wore pants, and now…now that it's cool, she's wearing shorts. Why?* The question rattled around in his brain.

Jeez, he noted, *I haven't been paying much attention to my fellow fan. I don't remember her with such long, light red hair…or so many freckles…or those full lips…or…or such glowing white and pink skin…or her yellow eyes. Don't you think I would have noticed yellow eyes?* he chastised himself. *Also*, he thought, *her hands are so delicate, and I don't recall her voice being so husky. And such effervescence. Damn*, he concluded, *how could I not have noticed that she's…she's…so sexy?*

The question exploded in his brain and stirred him below. *And she loves baseball, no less. Holy cow, I think I'm in love! And I'm going on a date with her after the game?* At this time, all Steve could think of were Lou Gehrig's immortal words: "Today, I'm the luckiest man on the face of the Earth." Steve couldn't wait for the game to end.

At the conclusion of the game, the two new friends decided to leave their cars and return to them later. They hopped a streetcar at nearby Kenmore Square on Boston's famous "T"—a descendent of the country's next-to-the-oldest subway system. A few stops later, they arrived at the famous Faneuil Hall at the Quincy Market, and then strolled to the nearby restaurant.

Nancy was unusually chatty—but then again, today Nancy was unusually everything. She poked and prodded Steve, and nudged and held on to him supposedly for balance. *How can women get away with that?* he puzzled to himself. *If I poked and nudged her like that she'd have slapped me for sure. Maybe it's because men have made women second-class citizens, reducing them to how they appear, disregarding their thoughts and feelings. Who can blame women for using the weapon of touch to arouse attention and garner favors for themselves?*

Nancy, it seemed to him, was devastatingly disarming with her touch, her arms so powerful yet hands so delicate. Steve was able to process all this rationally, almost coolly, until his knees buckled shortly before arriving at the restaurant, when she slipped her lissome hand inside his. *How could she clasp my hand with no embarrassment, no hint on her face that anything's changed? Just total confidence. He hadn't known until just this very moment that he would be putty in her hands. How could she?*

They climbed up the dark, steep narrow staircase to the famous second-floor Boston landmark eatery: Durgin Park, home for decades of the best prime rib and fish—and the surliest waitresses this side of Hell. It was all in good fun, but when the waitresses sneered and looked down their noses at you, it was unnerving nevertheless. The couple arrived onto the dark wooden entryway.

"You want to eat *here*?" the hostess snorted. "What makes you think there's seating for *you*?" There were at least ten booths available, but she sighed in mock disgust, "very well then, I'll go check on seating."

A waitress returned fairly quickly and impertinently ushered them into a booth by the window. "And I suppose you'd like *menus*?" Nancy and Steve both guffawed.

"No," Nancy retorted, "just bring us your best prime rib, medium, and a nice bottle of champagne. Price is no object, since he's paying," she pointed to Steve with a flashy smile.

"And what are we celebrating folks?" the waitress asked with feigned mild interest.

"The Red Sox," Nancy said raising her arms up high in a "V."

"The Red Sox?" the waitress and Steve asked together.

"Yup," Nancy responded, "the Sox are going to win the Series!"

"Will that be sometime this millennium, dear?" the waitress snickered.

"Yup," Nancy giggled, "in exactly one month," she said seriously.

"Well," the waitress said in an aside to Steve, "I think I'll hold the champagne. It appears she's already had too much to drink." The waitress then turned to depart.

"Oh excuse me, miss," Steve said getting into the swing of things, "aren't you supposed to put the napkins on our laps?"

"Whaddya think this is, the Ritz?" the waitress snarled. "Oh never mind, here…" The surly waitress, dressed all in stark white to match the table décor, snapped open Steve's and Nancy's crisp white cloths and laid them ceremoniously, one at a time, over their laps. Everyone laughed, including the people at the nearby tables.

"It's a good thing the food's so good here," Nancy innocently explained.

"Why's that, dear?" the waitress inquired.

"Because you can't say much about the service!"

The waitress laughed. "I'll have to remember that. That's a good one!" She turned on her heels and strode toward the kitchen to place their order. "I'll be right back with the champagne. Go Sox!" she said over her shoulder.

Steve was flabbergasted. Nancy was so comfortable in any situation—at the ballpark, with him—even turning this professional malcontent of a waitress over to her side. "I'm charmed," he said absentmindedly under his breath.

"What, Steve?"

"Oh, I, uh, did I say…" he mumbled as he snapped out of his light trance.

"You said something about being charmed, I think."

"I *did*?" he turned red.

"Why, if I didn't know any better, Steve, I'd think you're blushing! How cute!"

Placing his elbows on the table, he covered his face in his hands. Finally, recovered, he declared, "Oh, all right, dammit! I said you charmed me. I just now realized that, b-but…I was already charmed—a ballgame, a streetcar ride, and a walk ago."

"Oh, aren't you sweet, Steve," she exclaimed reaching over the table and clasping his hand. "See? God will eventually win. My days are doomed. It might take an eon, but in the battle of good and evil, God will triumph one day. The Apocalypse will not come. There's more God than Satan in you."

Afraid, Steve removed his hand from hers. "What are you talking—"

"Ah, the champagne," Nancy sighed with relief, and then added, "not a moment too soon."

"May I pour for you, monsieur et madam?" the waitress asked with a twinkle in her eye.

"Mais oui, merci," Nancy smiled.

With a flourish, the waitress poured the bubbly liquid into their refined crystal stemware. "To the Red Sox," she said as she motioned to the couple to hoist their glasses. All three smiled. The couple heard the waitress' voice trailing away as she walked off: "Red Sox? Ha! Series? Ha! World Champs? That's a laugh! They'll be lucky to beat the damn Yankees for the Pennant! Ha!"

The couple burst out laughing at the departing diatribe of their classic Durgin Park waitress. "Drink up, sweetheart," Nancy chirped.

"I think I'll wait for the roast beef," Steve responded.

"Listen, Steve," Nancy said with uncharacteristic sternness. Her face turned somber; her yellow eyes narrowed. "I'm going to tell you a lot of stuff now, and the sooner you realize that I'm not nuts, and the sooner you can accept that what I'm saying is not baloney, the sooner you can get over this next month and return to your normal life. To process all this, you'll need the champagne to cut through your screen of disbelief. Otherwise, you're going to spend an eternity in regret. Now drink, Steve…please," she urged. "Bottoms up." She made sure he started to drink and then drained her glass along with his. Quickly, she poured them both another glass. "Drink, Steve," she said firmly.

"Look, Nancy, I don't know what's—"

"First of all, sweetheart," she interjected, "I'm not Nancy."

Steve quickly scooted his backside up as high as he could against the wall at the end of his booth. "What…how…" His eyes fluttered wildly. He began to cough and choke.

She came over, sat beside him, and started to slap him on the back. "Are you all right? I think something went down the wrong pipe. Here." She thrust his champagne glass into his hand. "Drink," she commanded.

He slammed his glass down after he drank, and spoke with a voice of betrayal. "Water!" She handed him a glass of water, and he drank heartily. "Thanks," he murmured.

"I'm sorry this is so hard on you, Steve," she said softly, her hand now around his neck. She gave his cheek a kiss, sending sparks down his spine.

"Ah, have you lovebirds decided to get closer? I could rent you a cot in the back if you'd like. Only twenty-five cents a minute. It's real affordable for quickies," the waitress quipped.

"No, that's real nice of you," Nancy said with a forced gypsy smile that did not reach her smoldering eyes, "but I like to luxuriate in sex. Your bathrooms are fine, and besides they're free. Wanna join us there?" She finished by hugging Steve around his waist and bringing her cheek flush to his as he blushed.

"Well, I guess I've met my match," the waitress said, putting their plates in front of them, and moving Nancy's former place setting in front of her new seat next to Steve.

"No more Mrs. Nice Gal," the waitress warned.

"Is that what you call being nice?" Nancy cracked.

"Say," the waitress smiled, "haven't you eaten here before?"

"Yeah, many times, actually."

"Oh, so was that *you* screaming in the bathroom last week?"

"No, I'm pretty good now at muffling my screams of delight, but my friends...well, no matter how much I try to have them bury their screams in these," she said moving her bountiful chest back and forth several times, "they're sometimes out of control."

Steve jumped as Nancy squeezed the top of his thigh. The waitress rolled her eyes and shook her head before asking, "Which bathroom?"

"Oh, the women's of course. They're cleaner. What time do you get off?

"About nine-thirty."

"Well, come into the women's bathroom around then." She turned and said while cupping Steve's chin in her hand, "You up for a little ménage, eh Steve?" She turned back to the waitress and winked. "He's shy, but I've never met a man yet who'd turn down a ménage à trois."

"Well, bon appétit, mes amis, and I don't just mean the roast beef," the waitress quipped walking away.

"Come much after nine-thirty," Nancy cracked, pointing her thumb at Steve, "and there won't be much left of him either." The waitress gave a perfunctory wave of her hand in acknowledgment without looking back.

"Eat up, Steve," Nancy urged, "before your food gets cold. Do you like white horseradish on it? I love it that way."

"H-How can you be so…so nonchalant? You just told me you're not Nancy, and then you kiss, hug, and make me jump. I'm being accosted by a total stranger, and you're asking me if I like horseradish, as if we're an old married couple." His fluster mounted, and he spoke in rising tones, "For God's sake, tell me what the hell's going on. Where the hell is Nancy, and who the hell are *you*?"

"Well, you're not too far off with the Hell part, anyway," she responded under her breath. Okay, Steve," she turned in her seat to face him, her fiery eyes peering into his. I'll tell you everything, but you need to do me a favor, please."

"Okay," he said on the verge of tears, "but just tell me."

"All right. For the next ten minutes, though, promise me you'll pretend—just pretend—that everything I say is true, and that you're not crazy, and I'm not crazy. Can you do that?" she asked intertwining her fingers with his.

"Oh, cripes, Nancy, or whoever you are, my heart melts when you do that. I'll really try to pretend, I promise. I'll also go with you to the bathroom if you want, even—God help me—with the waitress."

"That's better," she smiled. "Does the ten minutes start now, sweetheart?" He nodded his head in rapt attention. "I'm not kidding about the bathroom. I might ask you later, and if you want, we'll go. And for you, it'll be as close to Heaven as you'll get…especially if the waitress joins us."

They both laughed easily. "Ah, that's really good, Steve. Now eat while I talk. This stuff tastes great." They both began to cut into their pink, tender meat. She poured him another drink.

"First," she began, "Nancy's fine. I bought her tickets from her for this game. She'll be at the Playoffs."

"Why?" he tried to ask with his mouth full of meat.

"Because you're the one. Look," she raised her finger to him, "don't keep asking why. I'll get around to all the why's, okay?" He nodded, sipping champagne she happily noted. "I needed to get to know you so I could bring you here—someplace, anyplace—so you could help to accomplish my master's plan. Don't ask," she reminded him. "My master is Satan. Maybe you know him as Lucifer or Mephistopheles?" Steve's face turned white as he again slid over to the corner of the booth as far as he could get from her. "My real name is Leah, but I've taken many other names throughout the past, oh, fifty-six hundred plus years."

"You said I was chosen. Why me?" he asked with sullen anger.

"Well, you were the cutest guy among all the rabid season ticket holders and, er, since I get real close to the chosen ones, I want to receive as much sensual pleasure as possible from the relationship."

"But, I don't *want* to be chosen," he said in exasperation. "My people have been chosen for thousands of years, and look where it's gotten us."

"Ah, you're Jewish. So that's why you're having a difficult time accepting all this. You don't believe my master exists…or even that Hell exists. Well, okay. Now I see the problem. But, remember, you have to pretend…"

"Okay, go on. But *I'm* pouring myself another drink!" he exclaimed.

Leah laughed and continued. The sun had set and darkness descended upon Boston. "Trust me," she said. "Hell exists, and I didn't want to reside there. I was so jealous of my beautiful sister, Rachel, so lovely, so passionate, while I…I was homely. The Bible calls me 'weak-eyed.' That wouldn't have bothered me so much, but Jacob loved her, head over heels, while I'm the one who bore most of his children from whom many of the Jews in the world are descended, including Moses, David, and Jesus."

"Including me?" Steve asked, mouth agape.

"Yeah, like you, Steve. I guess the lineage went all to Hell during the last couple thousand years," she giggled.

"You didn't have to be jealous, you know," Steve responded. You and your sister were two dimensions of love: She the tall bright flame of passion, and you the blue still water of devotion. Jacob needed both of you, and obviously while he was attracted to Rachel, he certainly must have had some passion for you because, gosh, you had seven of his nine children—not counting several others by your sister's handmaid, Bilhah, and your own…"

"Yes, Zilpah. A trustworthy slave if ever there was one. But even she was more beautiful than I. You're right, though, about my needless jealousy. Jesus, Himself, pointed that out to me, but," she paused taking in a long, deep breath, "only a few millennia too late to save me from my eternal damnation."

"What happened to you, Leah? Give me the midrash on your life."

"Well, more like a mishigas, actually," Leah sighed. Steve laughed, as he slurped down his last tender morsel of beef. "I died after giving birth to Jacob's last child, long after my sister passed on. Just before that, though, I said to myself that I'd give up my soul to have the stunning looks of my sister, when poof, out of nowhere, this dude shows up who says he could arrange for that…under two conditions."

"What were they?" Steve inquired, crawling out now from the corner of the booth.

"First, I had to do his bidding in carrying out certain, uh, projects, like what I'm doing now. The second was that I would have to have sex with him whenever—and wherever—he wanted, just like with all his other handmaidens and servants."

"You're talking about Satan? Your master?" She simply nodded with a solemn expression. "And what happens if you refuse to do his bidding?"

"He brought me to the gates of Hell and told me that I would reside in there for all time if I didn't willingly cooperate with him. Too scary for me, I tell you. But I found out, too late, that I'm still eternally damned, because since I gave up my soul I can't feel love. Although…" she started to say dreamily, "although I do feel affection every once in a while. That's what I was babbling about earlier, that Satan has an Achilles heel: People on the whole have more of God's good than Satan's evil in them, and they have free will, so they can choose good and evil; and even when they choose evil, they can repent and choose good again—at least while they're alive. But, when they sell their souls for superficial goals, like eternal beauty, they still have residual goodness that Satan can't seem to snuff out completely. That's why I can feel affection, even if I can't feel love. Eventually, this tiny flaw of goodness will defeat my master, although it might be an eon from now."

"Okay, so now you can tell me that you've been putting me on, and the waitress and everyone at the tables around us are going to have a good laugh at my expense, and then we can go to my place and make love. Right?" Steve asked hopefully.

"I wish it were so. You got the making love part right, but think, Steve, why would I buy someone's seat at a ballgame just so I can have a meal and a couple of laughs?"

"I-I...I don't know. Maybe you're sick and need help?"

She searched his face, admiring his deep brown incredulous eyes. "I wish I were, Steve. I wish that were true...but it isn't."

Steve sat in suspicious silence, then said, "Is there any more champagne?"

Leah chuckled and handed him the green bottle. Steve put the mouth of the bottle to his lips and polished off the contents. "I have a feeling it's going to get worse," he proclaimed, wiping his mouth with the back of his hand.

"Yes, but you're still not convinced, and ya gotta be shoo-ah," she said, imitating a New England accent for the word "sure." "I hate to do this to you, Steve. It scares the heck out of the chosen ones, but ya gotta be shoo-ah."

"What scares us?" Steve said anxiously licking his lips.

"What color are my eyes, Steve?"

"Why, they're that unbelievable yellow color."

"Would you like to see how I look with green eyes? Look at my eyes closely, Steve."

When he had focused on her, she blinked slowly and then opened her lids. "Oh my God!" he jumped. He was agog. "How...?"

"What's your favorite eye color of a woman, Steve?"

"I-I go crazy…Don't…don't do this to me, Leah, please don't…"

"What color?" she pressed.

"Oh, God, violet. I go crazy over women with violet eyes."

"Okay. Watch closely, my chosen one." She slowly closed and opened her eyelids.

"Oh, God!" Steve blurted out. People turned and stared.

"I told you, if you've got to scream, scream into my bosom."

"Let me see…" He moved his nose determinedly next to hers and scrutinized her irises. "Christ, they're real!"

"Do you like my freckles? Aren't they a little too dark for you?"

"Good, God," he jumped back for the third time that evening into the corner of his booth. "They're lighter! Your freckles are lighter!" he said in amazement.

"What's your favorite hair color for a woman, Steve?"

"Don't, please don't," he begged.

"What color, dammit!" she hissed at him.

"Blonde, blonde, okay blonde. Oh dear God, not again…you're…you're…you're *blonde*. How can this *be?*"

"Look, Steve, I can tell you still have a little doubt. You see the candle on the table?"

"Yes. It went out a while ago."

"Right. If I light the candle by simply pointing my finger at it, will you finally believe me, and listen to the assignment my master has for you?" Dazed, he nodded and opened his eyes wide. "Okay," she said, "watch as I point now."

Leah looked around the room making sure nobody was watching, and quickly pointed at the candle with her forefinger. A flame appeared instantly on the wick. Just as fast, Steve jumped back—for the fourth time that evening—into his corner, bringing his feet up defensively onto the seat, clasping both arms tightly around his knees. His curly brown hair stood up on end. His face filled with terror, heart pounding against his ribs. "You witch!" he blurted out with hushed intensity.

"Oh, how I wish that were so, Steve," she said softly reaching out to calm him.

"*Don't* you touch me. Don't you *dare*," he said with continued vehemence. Although the clanking of dishes and patrons' laughter filled the dining room, all the two could hear was silence. Slowly, his face softened as he continued to stare. She remained motionless to stem his inclination to scream or lash out at her.

Soon, Steve began to sniffle, raising his hand to his nose. His eyes turned red. He started to tremble. Unashamedly, a tear oozed out of the corner of one eye. He started to rock back and forth. His eyelids blinked ever faster as now a rivulet of tears swept down his cheeks. Rocking to and fro, he continued to stare through the mist at her. His eyes then scrunched shut and he covered his face with both hands. His body wracked uncontrollably with sobs.

In a high-pitched squeak, Steve began to call out "Leah!…my Leah! Oh God, you're Leah!"

He reached out for her and his crying became louder. She quickly scooted over and guided his feet to the floor. She reached around his back with one hand and held his head against her shoulder with the other. Alternately, she kissed his head and made soft shushing sounds through her teeth. "It's all right, sweetheart. Everything will be all right."

Finally, after many minutes, Steve calmed down enough to say, "It will never be all right, Leah. Things will never be the same for me again."

"Why, sweetheart?"

"Don't you see? You're my Leah, my Matriarch with a capital 'M.' "

Leah looked up at him with a start. "Oh, my God…ooh, I'm sorry, master. It's just a figure of speech. I didn't mean anything by it, honest!" She winced looking wildly all around, expecting her master to poof any second in front of her. After a while, she relaxed enough to say "Whew. Is it ever horrible when Satan appears. After all these millennia, I'm finally getting used to his sudden appearances. Now, I only dread the experience. The other poor schnooks—under five thousand years—experience abject terror." Both laughed nervously.

"Anyways, Steve, now I understand your reaction. I'm your foremother. I can't believe my master could have been aware of this possible encounter and still have arranged for a meeting between a Jew and his nearly most distant ancestor. You can't go back much farther than me in Jewish lineage, only to my mother, Rebecca—yeow, talk about gorgeous—and devious, my gosh—and to my grandmother, Sarah—not such a bad looker herself, and wise…wow, right off the charts. I can't believe my master arranged for this sacred encounter—with a capital 'G', if you know what I mean—with one of his own diabolic handmaidens no less. If he ever finds out, he'll have a fit. Anyone within a hundred miles of one of my master's fits is toast. Not a pretty picture, but…now that I think about it, it does beat going to Hell in a hand basket," she snickered.

When Leah finished talking, she realized that Steve had snuggled his face into the cradle of her neck, surfacing every once in a while to kiss her cheek tenderly. He was in a state of bliss, as close to Heaven, he imagined, as he'd ever get.

As he lay on her shoulder with eyes closed, arms wrapped around her waist, the waitress appeared. She started to say something when Leah raised and wagged her finger near her face. "Uh-uh," Leah said softly. "Not now." The waitress left the bill on the table. "Thank you," Leah cooed appreciatively.

"Take your time," the waitress whispered and tiptoed away. Leah then pointed her finger at the bill, and just like that, two hundred dollars appeared.

"Steve," Leah whispered, kissing him on his cheek.

"Hmm?" he intoned.

"Steve, don't you want to make love to me?"

He slowly sat up, unwrapping himself from around her body. "I already did," he said.

"What do you mean?" she asked completely befuddled.

"I already did. Make love to you, that is. I was in spiritual ecstasy. Total love. I skipped right over the petty sexual stuff, and had an orgasm of the soul. I'm sorry you can't experience that, Leah. It's indescribable. And besides," he said, seeming to come out of his trance, "we can't."

"Can't what? Make love?"

"Right, because we're relatives."

Leah leaned away from him and burst out laughing. "You're kidding! First of all, we're so many generations removed from each other that if we shared even one gene between us it would be amazing. Second, I hate to burst your bubble, but while I'm your spiritual matriarch, we're of different blood lines, I think."

"How the heck…?"

"Shh. Go back to resting on me. You adore. Leave the talking to me." He leaned his head down again on her shoulder. "Okay, that's better," Leah said. You're Ashkenazi, right? Your ancestors hailed from Eastern Europe?"

"Yes, White Russia, near Minsk, from Barbrusk," he said looking up briefly.

"Well, I was there in the 1500s when a tribe of Arabs migrated north and stayed in what is now Croatia. Over time, they converted to Judaism, and then migrated to Russia and Germany. So you see, my love, you probably came from the house of Ishmael—from where the Muslims descended—while I originally came from Haran, where Jacob came to my Uncle Laban looking for a wife—or two or more, Rachel and me, and of course Bilhah and Zilpah. Finally, even if we *are* closely related, look at our matriarchs and patriarchs. My grandparents were half brother and half sister, for crying out loud, and me, I was Jacob's niece. And besides, you and I aren't planning to get married or produce offspring, are we? And even if we were, in Massachusetts second cousins can marry."

"You are a seducer, Leah. You always were, I guess. And then, too, now you're outrageously gorgeous. Still, it does seem almost, dare I say, anti-climactic after such spiritual ecstasy, to share only physical lust. But, I tell you what, why don't we sleep on it. I'm plumb exhausted from this epiphany. You can stay at my place, unless you have a hang-out you prefer while wreaking havoc for your master in Boston."

"No," she chuckled, "your place sounds good."

"Meanwhile, you can tell me on the streetcar and at home what I have to do, and what the consequences are for my unwillingness—or ineptitude—in executing this…this diabolical project of yours."

"Failure to participate, or to succeed are not options for me, and are terrifying and terminal for you, Steve. So, let's see if you can finish this project without meeting Satan, hmm, shall we?"

"All right, Leah. Should I pay now?"

"Already taken care of," she smiled holding up her index finger and wiggling it for a few moments.

He looked back at the money on the table. "Ha! Why does that surprise me?" he asked rolling his eyes as the two paused to look at the staff photos on the dark wall before descending the stairs into the brisk fall moonlit air.

During their walk on the red brick pavement through the market to catch the return streetcar to Fenway Park, Steve asked how sex was with Leah's master. She explained how Satan often appears as an Adonis to his handmaidens because his appearance, as she said, "like that of Hashem, Yahweh, Adonai, Ein Sof, El, or whatever you call God nowadays, is unknowable, and would be frightening if he appeared in his "true' form." She explained that Satan is a fantastic lover, physically anyway, because he knows everything about pleasing, and getting pleased by, women…and yes, by men, too.

As she talked, Steve learned that Leah lacked love in sex with her master, and that's why she enjoyed sex with her chosen ones. At least with humans, she told him, she would receive a glimmer of hope for obtaining affection, something that Satan was either incapable or unwilling to give or receive.

"But you're different, Steve," she pointed out, sweeping her new blonde hair off her forehead to fall on her shoulders, "from all other humans in your adoration of me."

"Yes, that's because I'm Jewish and you're my foremother. So even though you're not divine, you're almost like a goddess to me, and not just in a physical sense. I would have the same love for you even if you looked like the weak-eyed Leah described in the Bible."

"You're the first person to feel that way, and I believe I might have actually felt your love back at the restaurant."

"Do you think so?" Steve asked excitedly.

"What do you mean? Why so excited?" she asked perking up.

"I don't know. Let me think about it, but maybe you have some vestiges of a soul in you. If so…well, let me think about what that means. It might be important."

They descended the steps to the underground subway stop in time to be greeted by the clanking and squealing of a streetcar — a progeny of the original cars over 110 years old — braking to a stop at the platform. Steve and Leah climbed aboard and found two seats together away from others in the near-empty car. She proceeded to tell Steve in a low voice what her master's devilish assignment was for him.

"You're not gonna like this, Steve, but here goes, okay?" He nodded, ready to be absorbed in her every word. He held her hand gently in his as she continued. "The Red Sox will win the Pennant and the World Series this year…but only if you don't see the games. Nancy can see the games, and I'll take your tickets and sit next to her."

"Jeez," he exhaled and stroked his chin, "the Red Sox will win and I won't be a witness to it? Well," he sighed in resignation, "I guess I could do that for the home team."

"Maybe so, but it's a little more complicated than that, Steve." He encouraged her to continue, as he stared in the dim light at her stunning porcelain white face.

"You see, sweetheart, you can't look at *any* moving pictures of any of the Divisional, League, or World Series games. That means no TV, no computer videos, and also no radio descriptions of the games. The only thing you can do is read in the papers about the results of each game. This means that if you even accidentally watch or hear the games—even a news program—the Sox will lose."

"Cripes," he responded with a great deal of consternation, "how is that possible? I'd have to avoid all radio and TV contact, avoid electronic media in stores and at work, and just not turn on anything at home. Cripes," he said again several times as he scratched his head and rose to pace the aisle of the streetcar.

Shortly afterwards, the two arrived at their destination and they made arrangements for Leah to follow Steve to his suburban home in their cars. They arrived at his small house together, parked on the legal side of the street, and made their way to his front door.

When they entered the house, he turned on the light. Just then, his face brightened and he snapped his fingers. "I know! I know! I'll take a vacation from work and just sequester myself at home."

"Bravo, Steve," Leah exclaimed, clapping her hands. "You truly are a dedicated Sox fan, and you do believe this whole situation."

"Yeah, well now would be a good time for the waitress to pop out of the closet to reveal your elaborate ruse."

"Yes, it would, Steve," she responded. Her eyes narrowed and she held up a wiggling index finger.

"Oh yeah," he said morosely, slumping into a living room chair, "how the heck could I forget?" It was his turn to harden his stare. "What if I don't cooperate, huh?" he asked defiantly. "Will you turn me to a crisp?"

"No, dear Steve," she said sadly, "my master will take care of that chore very quickly...and the Sox will lose."

In mounting anger he said, "So? So what? It's only a game."

"No, sweet thing, I wish it were so."

"What do..."

"Come into the bedroom and I'll explain. I promise, I'll explain everything. For thousands of years I've never had to explain all the details to my chosen ones. Never wanted to. Even enjoyed stringing them along and seeing my humans squirm a little. But you…you…I want to share everything and make this as painless as possible for you."

"Why?" he asked in triumphal tones, even as she led him onto the bed in the adjoining room, and began to remove his tennis shoes.

"Well, to a large degree, it's because you're Jewish. What're the chances of that happening?"

"Ah, let's see now," Steve began in deep thought. "I think Jews make up about, oh, two tenths of one percent of the Earth's population—enough to control the world, you know," he mused sarcastically.

"Point well taken," she said while slowly unbuttoning his shirt.

"That means you have…oh wait, you missed a button, you sedulous seducer…you have about a one in five hundred chance of selecting a Jew for your projects. Which means that you've probably already chosen other Jews for your satanic schemes, but somehow didn't know it."

She sat up wide-eyed. "What do you mean?"

"How many projects do you average a year, Leah?" She held up two slender fingers. *Why does her every movement fascinate me?* he wondered. "Well," he shook his head to clear his mind of her beauty, "two times fifty-six hundred years, that's a little over eleven thousand projects since you, um, converted. Crap! You've gotta be tired of all this."

"I can't tell you how much. But what's your point of all your calculations?"

"Oh, um, that means that out of your eleven thousand projects so far, ah, let's see now, twenty-two probably involved Jews."

"B-But, you're the first I know of," she cried out in disbelief.

"Yes, because even today there are Jews who deny their roots, or who just don't see Judaism as relevant to their lives. And you've lived through the last two thousand years, Leah. You've seen how revealing a Jewish heritage would often mean death to people and their kin."

"You're right," she whispered in his ear, languorously moving her fingertips through his thick black chest hair.

"Wait," he sputtered, putting distance between them, "you haven't told me everything yet. Spill it."

"Okay, okay. Look, if the Red Sox lose, you'll go to Hell, Nancy will die, and Iran will detonate a nuclear device on Israel."

"Shit! Damn you!" he exploded vehemently. "Killing me isn't enough? You have to kill an innocent bystander—someone I just happen to sit next to at ball games—and kill possibly hundreds or thousands...even millions of people in a country, and probably start World War Three to boot? This makes no goddamned sense!" he roared.

She let him rant and rave at the top of his lungs as he threw things and stomped around the bedroom. "Just get out, you witch!" His eyes became puffy, his face turned deep red. He tried to speak again, but instead burst into tears.

"Shh, my love. Come here." She pulled him into an embrace. He put his face in the cradle of her neck and cried, "Why, Leah, why? None of this makes sense!"

"I know. When you calm down, I'll explain." Soon he stopped sobbing and looked at her with tear-stained cheeks and hollow, red-rimmed eyes. "First of all, I'm only the messenger, the stupid, jealous idiot who sold her soul for skin-deep beauty, doomed forever to be a cog in Satan's evil plans. One of these days, I'll just tell him to throw me in Hell. But even then, I can't do anything to stop my master."

Steve only sighed and dabbed at the tears he wasn't able to choke back. "Second," Leah continued in a soothing voice, "Satan always has to gloat, always taking one more precious thing away than he needs to when he punishes people. That's why Nancy will die if the Sox lose. It's not enough that you die. Someone innocent you know has to die, too. Third, I assume you've heard of chaos theory?"

He nodded his head silently, and then spoke. "Yes, Einstein didn't like the theory much because he didn't think God would play dice with the universe."

"Right," she indicated emphatically, "but scientists said that if by chaos you mean probability, then it sounds like God's plan. So if something bad happened, like an improbable freakish accident, then we just cluck our tongues and point to low probability—bad luck you might say. In this way, Satan can link up events that no one could possibly dream of being related, like the results of a ball game and the dropping of a bomb, which reduces the possibility of anyone preventing the diabolical plan from occurring."

"Wow," he said half stunned, "your master's the ultimate terrorist."

"Yes, and in your case, a failure to carry out his assignment, resulting in a Red Sox loss, will lead to bedlam halfway around the world, and maybe, as you say, engulf everyone in a war."

"Christ!" Steve bellowed. "Armageddon! Bastard! How are these events linked, though?" he cried out.

"I don't know," she shrugged. "Like my former Master's plans, my current master's plans are ineffable, I'm afraid."

She let him rant and pace some more until he calmed down. Her violet cat eyes followed him with sympathy and admiration. "Are you ready, Steve?" she purred.

"Oh, Christ, I'm so tired and angry. I don't know what to do to ensure I succeed at this project," he said trying hard to refrain from blubbering again.

"Don't worry," she calmly reassured him, "I'll help you. Tomorrow I'll tell you how. Now, though," she commanded, "I'm going to give you the thrill of your life."

"I need rest," he said desperately, "not thrills."

"You can rest after I finish with you, or you can ravage me from pillar to post, whatever you'd like."

"You mean, whatever Leah wants…?"

"Yup," she interrupted, "Leah gets. You got that right."

For the first time since arriving home, Steve broke into a wide smile, and his eyes softened. "Oh all right, my dazzling beauty. Who can resist you anyway?"

"No one I've ever met in more than five and half millennia, sweetheart," she answered, meeting his embrace on the edge of the bed.

They kissed for a minute or two and disrobed each other with anticipation. "Holy cow!" he exclaimed jumping back a short distance holding in his hand her giant double F-cup bra. "I-I've never seen anything so…so…"

"So pendulous?" she laughingly suggested, while Steve sat helplessly staring at the flesh pouring out of her chest.

"What then?" she earnestly asked.

"So…so…voluminous," he said under his breath.

"What are you talking…"

"You're just…just so much. No, no…so *more*."

"What on earth…"

"You're just so much more than any other creature I've ever seen. Incredible. Way beyond beauty…or any words."

"Well, try, you sweet young man." Munificently, she held her sumptuous breasts toward his dazzled eyes.

Just then, some corny alliteration alighted on his brain, and he decided to share it with her. "You have miraculously magnificent mammaries, Leah. I'm sorry. I'm at a loss for any other words to describe your breasts."

Deep, diaphragmatic laughter emerged from her throat. He slowly crawled up to her and gently lay her head back on the pillow. He ensconced himself between her legs and reposed so his stomach lay on her pubic hairs. He propped himself up on his elbows and fingered her breasts with a feathery touch. "Mmm. Malleable, too. Miraculously magnificent malleable mammaries, my matriarch."

She laughed again gaily, and then admonished, "Okay, less talk now, more action."

"With pleasure, my princess," he responded. Ever so slowly and lightly he gave her breasts soft lingering kisses. He saw her eyes glaze over. She began to writhe…and then groan. "What's the matter, Leah? Am I hurting you?"

"N-No, I-I don't know what's happening," she said rising to lean on her elbows. "I haven't felt like this since…since I was close to Jacob."

"That's nice. I'm glad I can do that for you. Lie back down, sweetheart." He resumed his desiring kisses. She groaned louder as he moved from one node to the other. Her head twitched from side to side, her legs began to flail and lock over his, trying to propel him forward toward her groin.

"What's that, Leah?" Steve cried out suddenly.

Exasperation crept into her voice. "Damn! You're like a woman—always talking. *Now* what is it?"

"I-I don't know, b-but you're…you're glowing! There's a light above you, sort of like a halo, I think."

"What are you talking…Jesus, you're right!" she nearly yelled. "It even lights up the room. What the hell…" she began to ask in wide-eyed amazement.

"Cripes, Leah. Are you in love?" Steve asked excitedly.

"Y-Yeah. It's been so long, I can't remember, but I-I must be in love with you, Steve."

"I'm sorry, Leah." He bolted upright to a sitting position. "I'll continue my assault on your lovely breasts, I promise, but we've got to figure this out first. It could literally be your salvation, Leah."

"What do you mean?" Leah effused with confusion.

"I-I don't know, but this same light appeared each time there was true affection between the forefathers and foremothers, or whenever a foremother gave birth to a child. It was God's spirit or light, and it appeared always together with sexual love and birth, I think. I don't know the Hebrew—"

Unashamedly, she burst out loudly in tears, and it was Steve's turn to try to comfort an inconsolable Leah. "Shechinah," she finally whispered in perfect Hebrew, with the gutteral "ch" and the emphasis placed on the last syllable.

"Yes, yes, that's it! Shechinah, the Divine Feminine, entered into through sex," he exclaimed. "You've still got the ability for God to give you this light. Shechinah! You were right, Leah. All humans have at least an ember of a soul, but especially you, since you had a larger divine presence than almost all others to begin with. You just needed another soul who adored you for you, and not just for your flesh…although I have to admit, you are the most spectacular temptress on the planet."

"But what does that mean for us?" She pleaded for him to answer.

"Look, woman," he said in mock anger. "Enough talk. You'll tell me tomorrow how we can carry out your project, and I'll come up with a plan to thwart your master with your rediscovered power. But right now, I want to be God's instrument and see how brightly you can light up, and then I want to surround myself in your glory. Whatever happens, though, you can be sure I'll never again say the Avot prayer by mere rote."

"Is that the prayer where Jews invoke my name and those of the other founding mothers and fathers?"

"Yes, but I'm gonna say it like I mean it from now on."

"Well, Steve, say it with kavanah and ruach—with enthusiasm and spirit—as did Moses' sister, Miriam the prophet, when she led the Jews in the dancing and singing of the Michamocha prayer on the shores of the Sea of Reeds—to celebrate God's deliverance of her people—our people—from the Egyptians."

"Yes, my love," he said reverently, and promptly proceeded to romp with kavanah and ruach all over her body. With each passing orgasm, her divine light grew brighter, until the couple turned off the lamps in the bedroom and made love only by her glow. Before they slumbered in each other's arms, they came together in a deafening duet. For the first time in millennia, Leah realized she was experiencing feelings of love, peace…and happiness.

Steve prayed his violent spasms hadn't popped any blood vessels in his eyes and nose. He thought just before drifting off that he was going to move heaven and earth to save Nancy, stop a nuclear holocaust, and free Leah from the orbit of her Satanic sun. He could never imagine how people could give up their lives for a cause…until now.

Still, he wouldn't mind if the waitress sprang forth from under the bed shouting "Trick or treat, Steve, you've been tricked! Ha, ha! Happy Halloween! Oh, by the way, that was some lovemaking session. You both got nailed. Hoo boy. Why are your eyes so bloodshot? Maybe you'd better go wipe away the blood from your nose before you sleep. Ha, ha!" On second thought, Steve winced to himself before dozing off, the waitress can stay under the bed.

Morning broke brilliantly through Steve's bedroom window, first splashing light onto his fluttering eyelids, and then onto hers. He awoke with a start from her cushiony bosom. She stirred contentedly.

"Mmm, good morning, sweetheart," she purred.

"Good morning, love of my life," he responded, inching his way up to lock his lips onto hers.

"Wow, lion's breath. That's what comes from feasting."

"Yeah, were you ever the most delicious, quivering soft pink flesh and…"

She chuckled. "Okay, okay, I get the picture."

His morning organ swelled at the memory of it all. "Oh cripes, I'm hard. Didn't the waitress mention a quickie, or something like that?"

"She did, indeed," she affirmed.

"Would you mind terribly, dear?"

She burst out in gales of laughter. "No, knock yourself out, you pervert."

Oh, that's good," he snorted in reply as he scrambled behind her and opened her thighs. "She makes love with the lecherous Devil, and then calls *me* a pervert. Ha!"

"Wham bam..." she started to say.

"Thank you, ma'am," he finished. He gratefully kissed her neck and fingered her extraordinary nipples.

Through her soft afterglow moans she mentioned it was possible that Steve was a more consummate lover than even Jacob. When Steve said he found that difficult to believe, she reminded him that the major goal of sex in ancient times was procreation, and not so much recreation or expression. "Modern man," she also noted, "seems to be more considerate of how the woman feels, and wants her to explode with lust as he does. Finally," she concluded still between soft moans, "there are a lot less inhibitions today against exploring all orifices. Yesteryear, I would have recoiled in horror at Sodomic advances, just as Jacob would have been consumed with guilt had he tried.

Steve mentioned that Leah's glow, which had appeared during their quickie, had brightened again, after subsiding a little, when she spoke about the sexual practices of ancient and modern humans. "That means," he pointed out, "that just thinking about sexual love could bring you a spiritual visitation from God. That could be very important," he noted as he delivered a bone-crushing hug around her rib cage.

"Mmm, I can feel your love oozing into my pores," she murmured.

"And I feel your love so much, too. Look what you allowed me to do just now."

"You made me feel good, too, you know," she reminded him.

"Yes, but you didn't know I was going to do that. You would have let me spill myself into you without a care in the world about how you felt. You were letting me use you. You were servicing me."

"Ah, yes, that is one thing men and women of antiquity had. They lived in lusty times. Modern people have repressed this wondrous urge for the good of a complex society. I've observed the urban scene where anonymous sex and orgies are sad, futile attempts to regain this lustiness."

"Sad? Why sad, Leah?" he asked mournfully.

"Because it's lustiness combined with love that brings out the divine, my sweet. My only daughter, Dina, is a good example of this. A Canaanite prince raped her, but she won over his heart and they were to be wed. She would've had both lust and love in her marriage."

"What happened?" he asked sitting up at attention.

"I pleaded with Jacob to treat her kindly. Of course, I'm not mentioned in this part of the Bible, but Jacob blamed Dina for wandering around among the Canaanites. How the hell do you think Isaac found my mother, Rebecca, and Jacob found me? We were wandering around, that's how. Or else we'd never have met. Only brothers surrounded my poor Dina. She was just seeking female companionship, but for that she was blamed for her rape.

"Then," Leah angrily continued, "before Dina could enjoy marital bliss, my stupid, short-sighted and bloodthirsty sons, Simeon and Levi, slaughter all the men in the Canaanite village and drag Dina away."

The ensuing silence could have been cut with a knife. Finally, Steve spoke, softly caressing her face. "I'm sorry, sweet Leah."

"Ah well," she sighed. "Maybe it was for the best, because if my sons and Rachel's sons would have intermarried with the fertility-worshipping Canaanites, much of our heritage could have been lost. On the other hand, many of our prophets and kings, including David and Solomon, came out of the loins of my son, Judah, who moved away before all this mess with Dina happened.

"Please tell me about Judah," Steve implored.

"Well, I'll give you a nutshell version. Longer versions must come later, because all this talk about loins, well…makes me want yours."

"Jeez, you can say that again. Your halo's beginning to shine," he pointed out in delight. So hurry, Leah."

"All right. Judah had an incestuous affair with his daughter-in-law, Tamar, who disguised herself as a sacred prostitute so that Judah would want her. The result was twin sons whose begetting and begatting resulted eventually in the glory of Jerusalem."

"B-But…"

"Don't even ask, Steve," she said with a twinkle in her eye. "I'll just say for now that it probably had to do with Shechinah and the fact that Judah had broken an earlier promise to Tamar that would have left her childless with no status in any community. I say brava for Tamar because, unlike her wimpy foremothers—including me—who only prayed to God for children, Tamar took matters into her own hands."

"Hmm," Steve mused under his breath, "God helps those who help themselves, perhaps."

"What, sweetheart?"

"Oh, nothing. What you said made me realize that getting you safely out of the clutches of your master, while yet avoiding burning half the planet to a crisp, not to mention Nancy and me, is in our hands. If God likes what we're doing, He'll help. Otherwise…sayonara."

"Well, you love muffin, the only detonation I want right now," Leah pronounced as she tumbled Steve upon his back, "is you exploding in me."

"All right, you holy harlot," he said referring to the tale of Tamar as he pressed his palms into her bounteous flesh. They groaned incessantly. Her back arched. All of a sudden, she was snapped away by an eye-filling spectacle.

"Steve, Steve! Y-your g-glowing!" she stammered extensively.

"What the… Oh, my God!" He looked all around his head. "You're right. I'm glowing with…with Shechinah? How…"

"Jeez, Steve, a blessed union, maybe even a sacred one. Let 'er rip, Steve!"

He lay down again and played to his heart's content with her amazing chest as she gyrated joyfully. Her insides twisted, her back arched as before, her face contorted, and a shout leaped from her throat. Steve's scream pierced the air a few seconds later as he undulated wildly. In the early afterglow they smothered each other with kisses. They couldn't get enough of each other. Both glowed brightly.

"Wow, that was desperate!" Steve finally said.

"Amen!" Leah added. "If that's Shechinah, let me inside forever."

"Amen! But how is that possible? How could I get the glow?"

"Beats me," she shrugged. "Maybe God gave it to you because you're intimate and in love with one of His initial Chosen Ones? Or maybe you get it when you're emotionally open to another? I just don't know, my angel," she said stroking his dark curly locks as he combed his fingers through her brilliant gold hair.

"It doesn't really matter," he replied thoughtfully. "I can get the glow by being associated with you."

"Yes, that's probably true," she said with some assuredness, "because actually, in antiquity the glow didn't descend upon one person or another, but over the whole house. Of course, modern houses like this are large buildings on foundations, while even the chieftains of clans lived in relatively small tents pitched on sand. So the Shechinah descended over an entire tent when the person with divine presence, feminine or otherwise, was in residence."

"Gosh, I hope you're right. If not, the media and the fire department will be wondering about the glow over this house."

They both scrambled off the bed to look outside the window, and giggled with relief when, after craning their heads, they saw no glow near the roof. Meanwhile, their glows subsided, though not entirely so, until they were completely dressed.

Just then, Steve had a thought. "I've got it. You make breakfast and I'll tell you something that might be helpful to us."

"Okay, sweetheart," she said with cloying slyness that Steve didn't catch.

When they arrived in the kitchen, she pointed her finger at each side of the table, where scrambled eggs, toast, orange juice, and coffee appeared.

"Is any cream there?" Steve asked sarcastically.

She raised her finger again and a pitcher of cream materialized. "Anything else, your majesty?" He could only stare silently in wonder. "No? Well, let's eat. I'm famished. Start talking," she pretended to bark, "or do I need to spread the napkin over your lap first? My aim's not always that good in the morning," she announced with a gleam in her eye as she wagged her finger at him.

"No," he said quickly turning white as he covered his crotch with his hands while he sat down.

"Okay...mmm, this is good. Compliments to the chef," she said with her mouth full of egg.

"Yeah, thanks, Leah, this is great. Do you do windows?"

They chortled together, and then he began to speak at length upon her urging.

"Do you know the earlier Renaissance paintings showing the gold circles above people's heads to indicate halos? These frescoes, and then later oil paintings, were created by European and Byzantine artists like Giotto, who worked in the 1300s and 1400s."

She nodded her head taking a sip of her juice as he continued. "Modern people often make fun of these circles, believing that they are unsophisticated. However, most of the artists were Catholic, and I believe they understood and embraced the Feminine Divine. I think these artists were trying to portray their version of Shechinah, and not just a halo indicating sainthood or virtue.

"Yes, that sure makes sense," she marveled, "but what happened to the women in both Catholicism and Judaism?"

He went on about the irony of his comparison. "In Catholicism, the Virgin Mary elevated women to a very high spiritual status, yet in civil life, women were not accorded much respect. In early Judaism, the opposite occurred: While the religion turned away from the matrilineal and matriarchal societies to patrilineal and patriarchal societies, Shechinah was minimized and God was thought of in almost all masculine terms. Yet, in these male-dominated Jewish societies, women asked for, and were often granted, extraordinary civil and economic rights that didn't come to women in other segments of society for several millennia."

"Fascinating, Steve. Mind-blowing, actually. How does that help us?"

"Well, your master's world is almost totally masculine, so maybe its soulless citizens are shielded, if not immune, from God's masculine forces. But," he brightened, "maybe they're not immune to the feminine forces, chiefly the Shechinah. Leah, what do you think Satan could do to you if you were protected by the Feminine Divine?"

Leah looked perplexed before she spoke. "I don't know. I've never had the glow in my master's presence."

"Hmm. Do you think he could cast you into Hell, or make you a mortal again?"

"Yes, probably," she said sadly.

"But what if there were four our five of us all together with Shechinah protecting us?"

"I-I don't know. He might not be able to do anything. But his roar of frustration would be terrible to bear, and our fright might make the glow disappear."

"Well," Steve replied, "we're just going to have to trust that love—at least Divine love—conquers all."

"Who else could have this glow?" Leah urgently asked. "You?"

"Yes, but I'd have to be touching, or at least be very close to you, and that wouldn't be enough to repel the Devil. No, I'm thinking of the heavy artillery here," Steve said with eyes twinkling.

"Who? Don't keep me in suspense," she said excitedly.

"Your sister, mother, and grandmother, of course," he said with authority.

Her jaw dropped. "But how?"

"What do I look like, a magician?" he quipped. "I think the only thing I can do is send for them by praying to God to allow them to descend from Heaven at the exact time we'll need them to appear with their Shechinahs shining. You can't pray, Leah, since the Devil will hear you. I'll have to pray," he concluded with trepidation in his voice and his face.

"Do you know how to pray, Steve?"

"Not really, but I'll try to do what your descendent Hannah did, I guess. You might not be too acquainted with her because, well, she lived more than four thousand years after you died, Leah."

Oh yeah," she said sitting up straight, "Hannah prayed for a son, and had Samuel. She promised to offer him to the service of God, and she did, bringing him to Eli, the high priest, as soon as Samuel was weaned."

"Yes, but it's how she prayed—straight from the heart—that's important for me. In fact," he said in between sips of coffee, "because of Hannah, prayer for Jews became more central to the religion, making ritual and animal sacrifice less significant. But I don't know how I'm going to pray without thinking of you, my sardonic seducer."

Her face lit up in a smile. "Well, maybe that's good. You'll glow perhaps, and that'll catch His attention."

"No," he said more sternly than intended, "the glow *comes* from God's attention. It means He's *already* nearby. Don't forget that Leah. When your master angrily confronts you, your very salvation may depend upon it. To think otherwise, means you think you're already holy, when in fact you're holy only because God chose to bless you with the Shechinah in the first place. Please get that straight, Leah."

"A-All right," she said contritely, "I will, I promise, my love." He drank in her delightful vision, and a soft smile occurred on his formerly stern face.

Cripes, he thought, *I can't stay angry with her longer than a few seconds. She's Satan's Jewish handmaiden, beauty incarnate...and I'm hopelessly in love with her.*

"All right, Leah. You can come out of the doghouse. Now, tell me what I have to do to not watch or hear any of the Playoff or World Series games."

"Okay," she said leaning over, taking his hand in hers. She told him what he needed to do to stay home for a month as a recluse, including stopping his newspaper delivery, holding his mail at the post office, paying as many bills in advance as possible, and unplugging all the electronic media—radios, televisions, and "sorry, Steve, your computer and telephones."

"Telephones?" he blurted out rising from his seat. "Why?"

"Because my master is, shall we say, 'devilishly sly,' and he could call you and put a radio with the game on it up to the mouthpiece, and then, well, the ballgame's over...for Nancy and Israel."

"Me, too?" he asked sniffling, trying to stifle a tear.

"Actually," she responded, "I've never seen my master kill a chosen one when he or she valiantly tries to carry out the assignment and fails only because of being tricked by the master himself."

"So what happens to me, then?"

She rose from her seat, walked toward Steve, and hugged him before responding. "Nothing happens to you, my darling, except...except...you get to see the consequences of your failure."

"Oh God, a fate worse than death," he moaned, nearly collapsing sobbing into her arms. With Leah's comforting words and kisses, he eventually regained his composure. "What else do I need to do to prepare?" he asked resignedly.

She told him to arrange with his neighbors to receive and hold all deliveries, like UPS packages, and put signs on both front and back doors to make deliveries to these neighbors. She suggested that he give her a house key so she could bring in food and supplies to him, as well as the newspaper. She told him to tell his neighbors that one of his beautiful friends—"that's me," she beamed—would be coming and going into your house to check up on things. She also told him not to answer the door for anyone. "That's all you need," she admonished, "to open the door to the Devil disguised as your friendly postman, baker, butcher, or whatever, and be handed a radio with the game blaring away." Finally, she told him to bolt all doors and windows, and even close the flue to the chimney.

He expressed concern about how lonely he would be. She told him to stock up on as much reading material as he could, including any lessons he'd like to learn. "This would be a good time to learn Hebrew," she suggested, "or trigonometry or calculus. All the stuff you avoided in high school or college," she winked.

"But what about you?" he asked in a panic.

"I have, uh, many errands to do, but don't worry," she said with a wry lilt, "I'll be back every once in a while to charge up your batteries and drain your fluids. And who knows, if He's willing," she said pointing skyward, "we could shine up our halos. Mind if I stay here now and then?"

He laughed and tightly hugged her. "Could I stop you?"

She gently released herself from his embrace, and gave him a peck on the cheek. Then she turned away softly singing "Whatever Leah wants…" to the famous tune from the musical and film about the Red Sox nemesis. "You've got a lot to do, so get moving, Steve. What're you going to do first?"

"I think I'll go to the temple and pray."

"You could just stay right here, you know."

"Yeah, I guess so. That's the Protestants' gift to us: You can pray anywhere, anytime. You probably couldn't conquer the Frontier unless you were encouraged to pray by yourself until the churches could be built. But still, I guess I'm old fashioned," he said wistfully.

"No shame in that, my sweet," she said, as she picked up her pocketbook and headed toward the door. "The Playoffs start in three days, so I'll return in two days to see that you've done everything you need to do."

Steve handed her a house key and gave her an ardent kiss before she departed. He left shortly afterwards, his head in a daze, intoxicated with her and frantic about the potentially dangerous days ahead. He thought he would not take any chances, and so he walked to a nearby Orthodox temple.

Maybe Orthodox Jews are too wrapped up in rituals, he said to himself, *but at least they reserve their sanctuary as a sacred space. No social activities in sight of the Ark of the Covenant, the Ten*

Commandments, and the Eternal Light for them, no siree. Hmm, he thought, *I wonder what they think about King David dancing almost naked around the Ark? Well, I guess they'd think it was all right, since that was David's way of praying and giving thanks to God for His Covenant with His people.*

Opening the carved dark wooden door to the temple, the street noise gave way to noticeable silence. Steve found the sanctuary where he slid into a hard wooden bench near the front of the room. He blanched a little at the sight of the Eternal Light above the Ark lit with a bulb. *Jeez,* he thought, *I wonder if that's kept on during the Sabbath. Sacrilege! Well,* he softened a little to himself with a sigh, *it must be a fire law, an unavoidable tip of the hat to modern industrial life.* Steve knew that in Judaism the preservation of life takes precedent over any other Commandment.

"Well, enough of that," he said under his breath. *How should I pray?* he asked himself. He decided to think about *what* he was going to pray, then worry about *how* to say it. As to how to make his prayer come from his heart and soul, he could only hope that it would naturally occur if he could just quiet his overactive mind. For that, he began to meditate.

"Damn that Leah!" he exclaimed quietly. "I can't get her out of my head. A foremother of Jews…and so damn delicious." Suddenly, Steve stood up and angrily approached the Ark where the covered Torah slumbered between religious services. "Oh, God," he loudly implored, "how can I save Leah from the clutches of Satan? She wants to redeem herself. She sees how vain she's been and how evil her master is, and she's oh so tired of it. Please, God," he pleaded, spreading his hands out wide, "take her away from her evil associates and let her rest. Five and a half millennia is certainly enough punishment. A-And...Nancy. How can you let an innocent person die just because she's had the bad luck of sitting next to me all summer long...a-and being ignored by me just because I thought she wasn't good looking...or too quiet? That's no reason to die."

By this time, Steve had worked up a good head of steam. "And for crying out loud, how can You let thousands of civilians die, the people of Your own Covenant no less? But trust me, God, I'd ask You this even if the bomb weren't targeted at Israel. Aren't all people everywhere Your children? How can You help me to stop this travesty? Ya gotta help me, God. I need Your help!"

During the silence that followed Steve's outburst, he realized he had just wasted valuable time, ranting and railing at God. "Cripes," he said under his breath, "I've been here almost half an hour and haven't prayed yet."

"Who says, dear?" came the question from a seated figure near the rear of the small, dark sanctuary.

Steve turned, all flustered and red, to see a woman in a back pew. "Oh, I'm so sorry. I-I...You must think I'm nuts. Please forgive...oh, jeez, I'm really..."

"Who says?"

"I-I'm sorry, I don't understand."

You said you haven't prayed yet. How do you know you haven't?"

Steve stood speechless, rooted to the floor. She beckoned for him to come to her. In a daze, he haltingly ambled toward the rear of the sanctuary. He could see no reason to approach the lady; yet there was no reason not to, and if the person he offended by his outburst wanted to talk to him, he figured he at least owed her that much. With this thought in mind, he walked more resolutely to sit beside her.

He noticed that she was all dressed in white, and then he looked up into her face proclaiming "Holy cow! Y-Your…"

She burst out laughing. "You'd think that with the thousands of times I see this, I'd be used to it by now. But there's something about the human expression of recognition mixed with disbelief that's just so amusing to me. But yes, dear, I'm the waitress you keep hoping will pop out from hiding to tell you this is all an elaborate Halloween ruse. I'm sorry, Steve," she said lifting his hand sympathetically in hers. "I'd love to be able to tell you it's all a cruel hoax, but I can't…. it's all true, dear."

"But who…or what…are you?"

"I'm an angel, sweetheart."

"No," he almost yelled, pulling his hand away from hers. "This can't be happening! Why are you here?" he asked anxiously.

"You prayed for Divine help, didn't you?"

"No, I was just ranting and raving. I haven't prayed yet."

"Au contraire, mon ami, that was certainly one of the most heartfelt prayers we've ever heard. You asked for help to save an innocent person's life, to prevent a holocaust, and to free my poor foremother from Satan's grasp…and not once did you ask anything for yourself."

"But I didn't know…." Steve was thoroughly perplexed.

"Of course not, dear. People usually don't know when they've said a great prayer, because their conscious brains are basically resting at the height of their zeal."

Steve slumped over, stunned. He shook his head slowly in disbelief, occasionally pausing to glance at this Divine presence sitting next to him. He checked for clues—anything—to tell him that he was either dreaming, or that there were hidden cameras somewhere, ignominiously capturing him for the amusement of a worldwide television audience. After awhile, Steve asked gently, "Angel, does Leah know who you are?"

She simply shook her head back and forth.

"You know, Leah and I thought something was funny, because you weren't in any of the staff photos in Durgin Park's entryway. So why were you at Durgin Park anyway?"

"I think God could see Satan's incredible mistake in matching you up with Leah. He could smell an opportunity to thwart his errant angel and give him a good kick in the patoot—while giving you an opportunity for growth, too. He sent me to see if you would recognize Leah for who she is, and to see if she was ready to leave evil behind her. You did, and she is. Then God gave you two the Shechinah and you figured out its potential power against Satan. Finally, when you prayed, we knew you were the real deal…and He sent me to help you accomplish what you prayed for. You're very brave, Steve. I think Satan's betting on the wrong horse this time. It will be such fun for me to help put old Lucifer in his place, but terrifying for you…and Leah…and Nancy. But I'll help you all through it, I promise."

"Thanks, angel. Do I dare ask who you are?"

"Well, we don't have much time now for blubbering, but I guess a little more won't hurt you. All right, Steve. Here goes. I'm Esther."

He was agog, but then said, "No, how could that be? Esther was outrageously beautiful."

"Yes, I certainly was a breathtaking heartthrob, but I wanted the opposite of what Leah wanted. I wanted to be plain so that when I appeared to ordinary people, they would pay attention to what I said and not to how I looked. God thought that was rather noble of me and so granted my wish. He did a great job," she said smiling, pointing to her own face, "don't you think?"

Startled, Steve yelped, "Oh my God, Queen Esther, is that you?"

"Yes, Steve," she whispered.

His eyes turned to mist. *Oh no*, she said to herself, *here we go again*. He placed his hands over his eyes and bawled. His body wracked rhythmically to his sobs.

"Oh, all right," she said with only a little exasperation. "Come here, Steve. A little sacred time with another of your foremothers is good for you, I guess." She slid over on the bench and cradled his salty, tear-drenched face in her bosom, and fondled his hair and kissed him on the top of his head. "Shh, there, there, now, you have a good cry. Everything will be better in about a month."

Finally, Steve forced a weak laugh through his tears, and squeaked out an observation. "I guess you're the best angel for this project, Esther."

"How's that?" she perked up. "I'm listening."

"First, people talk about God helping those who help themselves. You didn't even ask God for help. You faced certain death because you were trying to save your people—my people—from annihilation. Without you, there probably wouldn't have been my people. And now, ironically, the distant ancestors of your Persian kingdom, the Iranians, are trying to complete what Haman and your husband, King Xerxes, were about to do twenty-five hundred years ago."

"Twenty-five hundred years ago," she repeated. "Wow, that makes me sound like a baby compared to Leah, doesn't it? It'll be great to have her join the fold. Her grandparents, parents, sister, and her children miss her."

"I know, and she longs for them, too. Can you really bring her to Heaven?" She nodded and he responded gleefully, "Oh, boy, wait'll I tell her."

"You can't, Steve. You can't tell Leah anything about this," she warned.

"Huh? Why not?" he asked in disbelief.

"Because the Devil will hear you, and then he'll be able to thwart our attempts to thwart him."

"B-But we're talking now about it."

"Yes, but I have the permanent protection of Shechinah, the same Feminine Divine that protected me from death in ancient Persia. You and Leah only have that protection sporadically."

"B-But…"

"Where's my glow?" she anticipated with a smile. He nodded. "Angels don't need a halo-like effect; but it's so rare and precious to humans, that God wants people to know where it is so that others can try to obtain it, too."

"But I've got to be able to tell Leah!"

"Well, okay, if you insist." At this time, Esther instructed Steve how to play a children's word game that would allow him to communicate with Leah without giving away any secrets to the Devil. "For some reason, maybe because of its innocent child-like quality, Satan has a deaf ear for this game," Esther observed, "and so people can speak about things that would otherwise cause the Prince of Darkness to rain havoc down upon them."

"Thank you, Esther, but what do I do now, my queen?"

"Just complete your preparations, dear, and I'll appear when you need me. Remember, though," she said in a serious tone, "you'll have to fail your assignment at just the right time. I'll tell you when."

"Fail?" he asked slapping his palm over his high forehead.

"Yes," she replied, "otherwise there wouldn't be any confrontation with Satan, and no chance to free Leah so I can take her to Heaven."

"I don't understand," he said sighing in exasperation.

"Of course not, dear," she smiled. "No one does completely."

"God does," Steve crowed.

"No dear, He doesn't."

"What!?" he said, completely taken aback.

She laughed. "I know that comes as a shock. People want to believe in the myth of Divine Omniscience. And in fact, God is omniscient, but He's not omni-empathic."

"I-I'm sorry, Esther," he said weakly, "you lost me there."

"I know," she chuckled, "but ontologically speaking, just leave it at this: Simply because God *knows* everything, doesn't mean He *understands* everything. For instance, while He admires your bravery greatly, He can't really understand it, because, unlike humans, there's nothing that God has to fear. Nothing can terrify Him, not even Satan. I think that's why He created angels who, like me, were once mortal. So while we angels are not omniscient by a long shot, we can nevertheless understand how you feel because we've been where you are."

"Wow, does anybody know this?" he asked wide-eyed.

"I think a lot of theologians and others suspect this, but only a few have mentioned this possibility because they feel such thinking would be considered blasphemous. But enough metaphysics for now. You'd better get going. You've a lot to do."

"All right, Esther my queen, but please tell me two things before I go."

"Okay," she said as she nodded her head.

"I-Is there sex in Heaven?"

"No, dear, there's no physical love in Heaven. We have what you experienced with me here and with Leah in the restaurant, what the ancient Greeks called Agape—pure love. You called it an orgasm of the soul, or ecstasy. That's pretty accurate as far as words go, although like most spiritual experiences, pure love is really ineffable. What's your other question, dear?"

"Tell me, Esther, are you going to bring Leah's relatives—our foremothers—with their Shechinahs down here to confront Satan at the appropriate time?"

"Hmm," she gazed off toward the Ark thoughtfully. "I hadn't planned on that, but you know, it's a great idea, Steve. I'll ask God when I have my weekly walk with him tomorrow. If He wills it, you'll have a chance to see your other early foremothers; although you probably won't have a chance to say hello, much less cry on their shoulders. We'll be too busy keeping you and Nancy alive to chit-chat."

"Oh, Nancy. Yeah, I almost forgot about her."

"You should get much better acquainted with her, dear. She's really quite lovely once you get to know her. Promise me you'll do that?"

"Yes, I'd really like to know her better. I think I'm going to need someone nice and sedate after this mishigas is over," he snickered.

"Great. You won't regret it. And now it's time to go."

"All right. Thank you Esther. May I kiss you?"

She laughed with a twinkle in her eye. "You are sort of diabolic."

"No, I mean on your cheek."

"Oh, of course, dear." Relieved, she slid over and gave him a hug while he planted a kiss on her cheek. Afterwards, she pressed her lips against his, and then disappeared…poof, just like that.

"Jeez," he gasped. "I hate it when things like that happen."

Just then, an elderly man in a disheveled trench coat walked into the sanctuary, and appeared startled. "Oh, I'm sorry," he said in a gravelly voice. "I didn't mean to disturb your prayer."

"No problem," Steve replied. "I just finished."

"Were your prayers answered?" he asked.

"Yes, as a matter of fact, they were." Before departing, Steve offered the man this advice: "Yelling at the Ark at the top of my lungs worked for me. Maybe it will for you, too. May Hashem respond to you favorably."

"He already has."

"How's that, sir?"

The man replied enigmatically "I am what I am." Then he, too, disappeared...poof, just like that.

Steve's knees buckled uncontrollably. He sat on a bench before he fainted. When he came to, Steve convinced himself that he must have imagined seeing God, but that Esther the angel was real.

At first unsteadily, Steve stepped out, disoriented, into the noisy city street, and walked toward home, bracing himself against the invading cold front. *Ah*, he thought, *the Sox pitching staff does well in chilly weather.* By the time he reached home, he had planned in his mind how he would accomplish all the steps Leah said he would need to take to prepare for his potentially month-long siege against the onslaught of media that is taken for granted in modern life. *Heck,* he thought, furrowing his brow, *the media actually might* be *modern life.* He shuddered to think what kind of withdrawal symptoms he would manifest when he unplugged himself from the wall. Strangely, he found himself looking forward to the experience.

During the second evening of Steve's preparations, Leah suddenly appeared with a poof. "Jesus!" he snapped. "I hate that. Can't you just use the key and walk through the door like everyone else? Even walking through a wall would be better than that."

"Sorry, my love," she said seriously, "you need the training. What I just did was nothing to what you'll feel if my master ever appeared before you. You need to learn to tolerate this kind of unexpected entrance." Leah then began to poke around the house and returned to Steve in the living room to compliment him on how thoroughly he had followed her directions.

"You even cut the plugs off all the electronic media."

"Yeah, no use taking any chances that someone might poof in here and plug something in for my listening or viewing pleasure."

"No," she laughed, "I guess not. So tell me," she said changing the subject, "were your prayers answered yesterday?"

"Oh, I dunno," he responded nervously.

She eyed him through narrow slits and approached him. She grabbed his ears and tilted his eyes down toward hers. "You're holding something back. Now, as you say, spill it," she cajoled.

"I-I...Leah, remember in the restaurant you asked me to pretend?"

"Yeah. You want me to pretend? Now?"

"Yup. Let's play a children's game, okay?"

"Sure, why not?" she smiled. He silently wrote the rules told to him by Esther on a piece of paper: *The third word in a sentence is the first word in your real sentence. Every third word after that is the next word in the real sentence.*

"Okay, wet's pway," she lisped as they laughed heartily together.

His coded sentences told her that he imagined God appeared in the form of an old man who looked and sounded strangely like George Burns. "Probably just nuts of me, though, huh?" he concluded, hoping Leah would agree.

Instead, Leah backed up, her mouth agape. "Oh crap!" she exclaimed. "Look!" she said pointing to above his head.

He turned his eyes upward and interjected with "Wow, I-I'm glowing!"

Leah started to speak when he sternly reminded her with, "The game, Leah, remember the game."

Haltingly, her coded sentences told him that he must have seen God. Otherwise, such a glow could never happen to him. Continuing to speak in code, they carried on the following conversation:

"That must have been a heckuva prayer, Steve."

"Yes. One minute I'm yelling at the Ark, and the next minute an angel—our waitress from Durgin Park, no less—is praising me for a great prayer."

"Whaaat? Crap! I practically told her to shut up in the restaurant. Jeez, and she still wants to help me? Who is the angel?"

"Queen Esther."

Leah sat down in a daze. "Very appropriate, given the Iranian situation. How will she help us?"

"At just the right moment, she said she would help you to reach Heaven to join your relatives, keep me and Nancy alive, and prevent the bombs from flying."

"Whew," she whistled. "How?"

He shrugged with upturned hands. "Beats me. But it'll require a confrontation with your underworld king."

"How?"

"She'll tell all of us what to do at the appropriate time."

"Damn," she said in amazement. "Do you suppose there's sex in Heaven?"

"I already asked her that."

"I'll bet you did. And?"

"There's no physical love, only pure love, like the kind I experienced with you in the restaurant."

"Huh! I suppose I could get used to that," she said without benefit of coded sentences. "Well, I guess we'd better sow your seeds while the sun's not shining, my love."

"Lead on, my delectable sex goddess."

They walked hand-in-hand into his bedroom, where Leah playfully explained a lovemaking technique. "The secret to undressing your partner is to allow him or her to finish taking off one article of clothing while you begin to take off another. See? I'm unbuttoning your shirt while you step out of your pants."

She slid one arm out of his shirt and let it hang off the other shoulder. As Steve extricated himself from the shirt, she deftly dropped his briefs to the floor.

As their divine glow lit up the room, she turned off the nearby lamp, and then surrounded Steve.

Silence ensued after their lovemaking. Finally Leah spoke. "You've taught me something important, my supreme lover. In my ancient days, couples usually were virgins when they married, and were often strangers to each other. So the fire of love, if it occurred at all, was ignited from the first sparks of intercourse. Modern people, especially you, have shown me that all aspects of intercourse, including the most devilishly delightful practices, like bondage and dominance/submission—and even sado-masochism—are wonderful within the context of love and mutual consent. Outside of love, these devilish practices are tantamount to rape. Inside, the Devil's own worst tools can be subverted for love, if we can but figure out how…"

"Yes, and if we don't sell our souls before at least trying to figure this out."

"Amen to that, brother…amen." Then she began to groan. "What *are* you doing, you devil?"

"You taught me something, too—surprise your lover by beginning a new titillating activity before a previous activity is completed. In this case, while you were finishing your revelation, I began to suck your spectacular breasts. It seems that nothing gets your juices jump-started more than being a captive of your own surprise. And now, if you'll excuse me…"

She responded with moans, gasping for breath and arching her back, before surrendering to the swaying and shuddering of her body.

"Oh cripes! Now look what you've made me do. It's all over your sheets, Steve."

"I don't mind, my pet. I want our mingled love juices on my sheets forever, to remind me of us."

"Oh, you're just too wonderful for words. Lie and rest on me, sweetheart. If you wake during the night, regardless of the time, please give me a quickie. Promise?"

"Yes, with pleasure," he murmured. He crawled up to place a soulful kiss on her curvaceous lips, and then slid down. Placing his head on her soft chest, he closed his tired eyes.

She asked herself, *did I really invite the angel to have sex with us? I can't believe I did that!* She laughed lightly and then gratefully, too, succumbed to sleep.

After a morning quickie, followed by a sumptuous breakfast—compliments of Leah's magical index finger—she announced to Steve that this was his first day of isolation, the first day of the baseball Playoffs. She admonished him to be vigilant and to not answer the door for any reason. He gave her a big hug and an ardent kiss, and she promised to return in a few days and bring him a newspaper, "and some fresh batteries and a siphon," she said with a naughty wink before disappearing as he settled into a chair to decide what to do with his idle time.

The first several days of solitude passed uneventfully. Although Steve didn't know it, the Red Sox breezed through the divisional series, sweeping the Anaheim Angels, setting up a match with the legendary Yankees. After ten days—or maybe it was eleven—he could not tell—he began to masturbate to the images in his head of the lovely Leah. Suddenly, he jumped at the unexpected appearance of the Devil's handmaiden.

"Jesus!" he gulped.

"No," she cackled, "it's only me, Leah. I couldn't let you spill your seed like this, and I've been hungering for you, too."

He groaned, "How I missed you. Oh God you're too much," he yelled. "Damn that felt good. Thank you, Leah, my beauty!"

"You're welcome, my worshipper." She told him he could have her again later, but that now she wanted to put away the food she brought with her. They quickly dressed and he followed her into the kitchen. She put groceries away and tidied up the dishes, the stove, and the refrigerator.

She was startled at his sudden outburst: "Jesus! What the…how could…how the hell…shit!" He paced aimlessly, red-faced, around the kitchen reading and re-reading the newspaper headline: *Yanks 3-0 Lead Insurmountable.*

"For Crissakes," Steve said apoplectically, "the Red Sox will lose. How the f—" he choked back the words. "Leah, no baseball team has ever come back to win four games in a playoff series after losing the first three. Hell, no team has ever even won *three* games after losing the first three. How can this be? Did I do something wrong? Did I see or hear something I wasn't supposed to? Tell me. What?" he asked vehemently, leaning down to pound the kitchen table.

"I don't know, dear," she chirped gaily. "I wasn't here."

"Don't play with me!" he glowered and growled at her.

"Oh ye of little faith. Okay, I'll tell you. I've seen my master, and he's decided he's tormented Boston long enough, so he thought he'd cause some grief in New York, and give their beloved Yankees the title of greatest choke in sports history. And that's what they'll have when they lose the next four games to Boston."

"Oh, how I wish I could be there to see that! I'd like to see the anguish in their fans' eyes for a change," he uttered gleefully.

"Ah, that's the Steve I know," she said relieved. "Just don't throw it all away now by doing something stupid."

'I won't," he said embarrassed. "I'm sorry I blew up at you."

"No need, dear." She hummed a few measures of "Take Me Out to the Ball Game" as she finished up her chores. "Oh, by the way, handsome, I think your friend, Nancy, likes you."

"Really?" he asked at first brightly before inquiring in more subdued tones, "Oh, I mean, really?"

"Yes," she laughed at his clumsy, flustered attempt to veil his initial reaction.

"How do you know she likes me?" he asked suspiciously.

"Oh, I just innocently told her you missed her."

"You did whaaat?" he cried out.

"I said—"

"I heard what you said," he snapped. "And what did she say?" he asked pretending disinterest.

"Who, dear?"

"Who the frig do you think I mean? Nancy, that's who," he said with a great deal of vexation. "You're killing me, Leah, you know that don't you?"

"All right, I'll tell you," she said suppressing a smile. "Nancy said she missed you, too."

"What!" he responded. "Oh no, you didn't. How could you—"

Interrupting, she said, "I simply explained to her that you had to go away on business, and that you hoped to return by the end of the World Series. Of course, she thought I was a complete nut case, since everyone knows Boston's losses are too many to overcome, and that the World Series will have to wait another year to host the Red Sox. I told her that when she sees me seated next to her at the start of the World Series against the Cardinals, she'd listen to me. When she asked me how I knew the Cardinals, and not the Astros, would win their League, I told her it was the same reason I knew the Red Sox would eventually overcome the Yankees. When she asked me again how I knew all this, I told her the Prince of Darkness himself told me so."

"Ha! She must have thought you were looney. But what did she say about me, huh?"

"Hmm," she uttered with mock jaundiced eyes, "methinks you like the lady."

"Well, if we both survive this ordeal and part company," he said with a trace of sadness, "I'm going to need a nice quiet, sedate companion. Besides," he teasingly noted, "she is sort of pretty."

"Oh, I'm jealous already," she said in feigned irritation.

"You needn't be," he said as she noticed his sudden seriousness. "I'll love you forever, Leah, but you've enlarged my heart, so I'll have space now for another who dwells on earth, since after this project you'll be untouchable to me, whether you go to Hades or Mt. Olympus."

She signified her understanding by nodding her head slightly several times.

"So what else did you tell her about me?" he asked excitedly.

"Oh, nothing much, just that you're fiercely loyal, and that you'd give up your life to save hers. That's when she said—with a faraway look in her eyes, I might add—that she missed you."

"Jeez, you're worse than your master, Leah. What a devil you are!"

"Not really, sweetheart. You see, that's the beauty of triadic relationships. The go-between—me in this case—can stretch the truth and also say complimentary things about the other two—you and Nancy in this case—that you can't or won't say to each other. In this way, incipient romances that might otherwise never materialize are forged."

"Well thanks for the sociology lesson. In other words, the roles of yenta and cupid occur frequently in everyday interaction."

"Bravo, very well said. But now it's time for action; specifically, you making love to me," she said playfully.

"I am. Don't you feel my foot rubbing your leg?"

"You call that making love?"

"Yes, ma'am. Every square inch of me is going to explore every inch of you so excruciatingly slowly that you won't be able to stand it." With that, they eagerly raced to the bedroom where they glowed all night, beside themselves with love and lust.

The uncertainty of the next few days of isolation induced Steve's nagging anxiety. He figured Leah, or even Satan himself, would have contacted him if the Red Sox had lost. Still, he couldn't help worrying about the possibility that Nancy and he might be spared harm because he had taken all precautions against hearing or seeing any electronic news about the games—and yet, the big bomb might right now be on its way to Israel.

Heck, he thought, *Armageddon could be taking place this very minute, and I wouldn't even know it.* He thought about the passage in the Torah that captured the opposite realization of Leah's then-future husband, Jacob: "This place is sacred and I didn't even know it."

In his own case, Steve thought the reverse might be true: he might be in Hell and not even know it. He laughed out loud at how his situation at this moment was so strikingly the reverse of Jacob's. In the latter case, Jacob was horny as heck and wanted intercourse, whereas in his own situation, his sex was glorious and often—with Jacob's former wife, no less! And yet, he could be in Hell, while Jacob wrestled with God near a ladder leading to Heaven. *Go figure!* he said to himself smiling broadly. He shook his head in wonder at this irony.

Soon afterwards, Leah appeared. Immediately, Steve shared his insights about the reverse parallel situation between Jacob and himself.

"Cripes, Steve," she blanched, "when you put it that way, I sound like an adulteress."

He was about to laugh when he saw the front page of the paper she had just dropped onto the kitchen table. "No way! Good God!" he proclaimed. *Impossible Comeback: Sox Win Historic Series 4 to 3* screamed the headlines.

"What's the matter, Steve, are you ill? You look a little green around the gills."

"I-I don't feel well." He stumbled forward and plopped into a chair.

She quickly brought him a glass of water. "You didn't really believe all this was true, did you Steve…until just now?"

"N-no. I-I…oh jeez. Deep down I was hoping this was all just a dream or an incredibly cruel hoax."

"How's that possible? Me lighting the candle with my finger, me changing my hair, eyes, and freckles, me making supper appear instantly, me making sublime love to you, you meeting your 'friends' in the temple, the glow of the Shechinah on you and me—how could you not think any of this was real?" she asked in amazement.

"I really don't know," he said meekly. I'm so sorry, Leah. I didn't mean to doubt you. I-I couldn't help it," he said trying—unsuccessfully—to choke back his tears.

Leah pulled up a chair and sat beside Steve. Holding him tightly, she murmured consoling words into his ear as he wept. When his tears stopped, he kissed her cheek lightly and then whispered "What now, sweet Leah, what now, my love?"

"Simple," she responded. "Wait it out until the end of the World Series."

"I wish that were true," he said in anguish. "Remember the game we played last time?" She nodded. In the coded language of the word game, Steve explained how the only path by which she could gain her freedom to join her relatives in Heaven was directly through her master, which meant that he, Steve, would have to violate the rules of his isolation. "How…?"

He raised his hand to silence her. "One of my friends in the temple, as you refer to them, will tell me when and how. Since this involves you, you'll have to stop by here each evening to stay in touch, just in case I hear from my 'friend.' Do you trust her? Do you trust me?"

"Hmm, I guess I'm in the same boat as you. You finally trusted me, so I guess I'll have to trust you." Then she continued in code to conclude, "The worst that can happen to me now is that I burn in Hell for eternity. Hineini!" she shouted in Hebrew to the sky.

Yes, dear," he responded softly, "I do believe you are prepared. You're ready. Whatever happens though, my Leah, remember: I'll always love you."

They both moved together into a strong embrace as they swept each other off their feet. The glow shone around them while their heads connected with a kiss.

Except for Leah's nocturnal visits, the next several days evolved uneventfully for Steve in his cocoon. Finally, soon after the sixth game of the World Series, Esther poofed in from nowhere.

"Jesus, you scared me," Steve yelped. Can't you angels knock like everyone else?"

"Sorry, Steve, but you wouldn't have answered the doorbell, even if I told you it was me, Esther."

Oh, right, yes of course." He recovered gradually from his fright. "What do I have to do, my angel?"

"Both you and Leah will need to be under the grandstand tomorrow during game seven behind home plate at Fenway Park."

"When?" he anxiously inquired, and licked his lips.

"At the bottom of the ninth inning. Here," she said holding out to him a small battery powered radio. "Go ahead, take it…but don't turn it on until about ten o'clock tomorrow night outside the ballpark. Then, when you hear that the Red Sox leadoff batter is coming to the plate in the ninth, you enter the ballpark, but not before, understand?" He nodded and she continued. "Leah should come in by herself and meet you, and then she needs to get Nancy and invite, cajole, carry…whatever she needs to do to bring Nancy to you. The three of you just wait there for further instructions from a messenger. I believe his name is Mr. Burns."

"Y-you don't mean…?" he stammered turning white.

"Don't ask. Just do whatever he tells you. I may or may not be there depending upon *my* instructions."

"Will Satan be there?"

"If he doesn't show up to confront you, he'll forfeit, and I've never known him to give up a chance to create havoc and death without a mighty fight."

"W-Will it be scary, my angel?"

"Yes, Steve." She reassured him by holding his hand. "But the success of your mission will depend on you regaining your composure and receiving your Divine glow. Just concentrate hard on how sexy Leah is and your halo of light will appear to protect you from Satan."

Esther gave Steve a strong hug and disappeared...just like that. He jumped with a start. *Damn,* he thought, *how I hate that!*

Later in the day, Leah appeared in Steve's home. He excitedly showed her the little radio, and speaking in code, he related the entire story about Esther's visit, and what he and she had to do the next evening.

"I know that look, Leah. You don't trust me, do you?"

"I-I guess not. I'm sorry."

He laughed softly. "Well, I don't either, but...I do trust Esther. And if you don't, then ya gotta at least have faith in Mr. Burns," he snickered.

"Mr. Burns?" she inquired quizzically.

"Never mind," he said with a dismissive waive of his hand, "I'll explain later. Meanwhile, I'll see you tomorrow night at the beginning of the ninth inning. Don't be late," he admonished her only half in jest.

With the shared realization that this night might be their last together, the Devil's handmaiden and her chosen one made love with fervor; yet, they were on edge and anxious about the danger they would surely face the next day. While spooning, they went to sleep after a short, intimate conversation:

"I'm sorry, my precious Leah."

"There's no need. I'm so glad I chose you, sweetheart."

"Yeah, me too. You're the best thing that ever happened to me. I'd give my life for you, you know."

"Please don't," she pleaded in anguish. "I've endured five and half millennia of this, and I'd gladly do it all again to know that you were safe."

"No," he said in code, "you have a chance to become an angel…I'm only a person, a mere mortal."

"Yes, I know, dear," she resigned herself to his resolve, "but most miracles occur here on Earth. As it turns out, humans are the most important angels of all."

"I suppose that's true. Either way, though," he said in a weepy tone, "I'm going to miss you so unbearably much, Leah."

"Shh, dear. Go to sleep. It's going to be a long day. I'll be gone in the morning. See you tomorrow, my sweet." The lovers went to sleep in a mutual glow.

Steve awoke, alone, with a sense of dread. Everything seemed to move slowly. His breathing was shallow and labored. His hands became clammy. It was an effort just to dress and prepare his meals, which, due to his loss of appetite, he left practically untouched.

In the evening, Steve couldn't remember how he arrived at the ballpark. He couldn't recall driving or parking, or even walking to the field. At ten o'clock, outside of the grandstand he flipped on the radio as instructed. When he turned the dial to the station broadcasting the game, a blinding flash of lightning accompanied by a deafening clap of thunder marred his senses. His hair stood on end, and he thought he heard the rumble of a voice saying, "Ha! You couldn't wait one more inning! You lose! You're mine now!"

Steve shook his head, trying to clear his brain. He heard the radio announcer introduce the Red Sox batter at the bottom of the ninth, telling the listeners the Cardinals were leading the Sox four to one. At this signal, Steve stumbled, completely disheveled and white as a ghost, into the park behind home plate. He hadn't remembered ever being more scared...until Leah appeared suddenly, and he jumped three feet.

"Steve, you look awful. Are you all right?" she asked concerned.

"I-I'm...no, actually." He told her about the thunder and lightning and the rumbling voice.

"Yup, that's Satan, all right. He loves to disorient his victims and drive them crazy before making a grand entrance."

"Shit, can't wait," he sneered sarcastically. "You'd better get Nancy before that bastard kills her. Remember, Esther said to do anything you had to do to bring her here."

"Right. Be back soon," she responded, and then ran up the stairs to the stands.

While Steve waited, he observed a monitor hanging from the stands above him. He noted that the Red Sox leadoff batter had walked. Then he perspired, despite the chilly, damp fall air, worrying about how Satan would appear to confront him. *Well,* he thought, *he had taken the best from this whole situation, now it was time to experience the worst.*

Leah bounced down the stairs carrying Nancy in her arms.

He gasped in shock. "Christ, is she *dead?*"

"No, she wouldn't believe who I was and how her life was in danger, so I knocked her out. I had no choice."

"Dear God! You *hit* her?"

"No," she answered, placing Nancy gently onto the cement pavement, and then holding up her wiggling forefinger. He could only hold his head in one hand and shake it in disbelief.

"Quick," she commanded, "kneel in front of Nancy and stay behind me. He's coming!"

"Who?"

"Who do you think?"

"Oh, crap!" he exclaimed.

"Yeah, that reminds me, try not to soil your pants."

Just then, a loud crack of thunder and searing light and heat ascended, it seemed, through the pavement. When their eyes adjusted from the shock, a monstrous evil creature—a behemoth—with lizard-like scales, green reptilian eyes, and a long twitching tail towered twenty feet above the three hapless figures.

"Angel, where are you?" Steve cried out in a terrified scream.

A loud grumbling voice like the Tyrannosaurus Rex in the Spielberg movies shot forth through gleaming razor-sharp six-inch teeth: "You insignificant maggots. You're mine now, all of you."

"Master," exclaimed Leah, dropping to her knees and bowing down, "I have failed you. Cast me down to Hell for all eternity, but leave these insignificant souls here. They're nothing to you."

"I am going to miss you, my favorite handmaiden," Satan shot back, "but you all go as a package deal—and I can't wait until the bombs drop, too." He followed up with a deafening fiendish cackle.

"Leah, can't anyone see us?" Steve whispered intensely.

"No, the Devil makes himself and his victims invisible, but that doesn't mean he couldn't burn an innocent bystander to a crisp right now by sending out fire through his nostrils and eyes…just to scare the crap out of us."

Nancy began to stir. She sat up, screamed at the sight of Satan, and fainted when he spoke, "It's time, you incompetents."

"No, not yet, my Prince," Leah reminded him. "You have to wait until the game is over and the Red Sox officially lose."

"A mere technicality," Satan bellowed, "but even you peons can be right now and then."

Although Steve was cowering behind Leah, he heard the noise from the fans increase in volume. He peeked out at the overhead monitor, observing that there were two outs and the bases were loaded with the Red Sox cleanup batter coming to the plate. *Boy, I wish I could be in the stands right now,* Steve said to himself. *This is about as exciting as it gets,* he thought, *even though the Sox have to lose.*

"Who says they have to lose?"

"Huh?" came the response practically in unison from the Devil, Leah, and Steve.

"Mr. Burns! Omigod, Leah, it's George Burns," Steve pointed and yelled.

THE RED SOX AND THE DEVIL'S HANDMAIDEN

The diminutive old man in a trench coat with heavy black-framed glasses took a cigar out of his mouth and spoke with a New York accent. "I could get you out of this situation if I wanted to, Steve, but in order to grow you need to face your fears directly. Didn't Esther or Leah tell you that I help those who help themselves?"

Steve trembled at the realization of who was speaking to him. Tears involuntarily gushed forth down his face, and he lay prostrate before Him. "Hashem, I'm sorry I doubted you!"

"Please, Steve." He knelt beside Steve and gently prodded his arm. "Get up, Steve," he said softly. "Sit up and listen a minute." Steve immediately did as instructed, gazing a tear-stained face into His. Steve received Hashem's message telepathically; for everyone else, time stood still:

"I don't give a damn if you doubt Me or don't believe in Me." He continued softly: "Hell, I don't even care if you pray to Satan here. If you must, you can extol my virtues during your religious services, and even now and then bow to My Torah and other sacred texts. You humans seem compelled somehow to do that. But in the end, all I care about is people treating each other justly. All else that's good in this world—truth, peace, beauty, friendship, wisdom, love, compassion, knowledge, mercy—everything—all of it—everything of value, both sacred and profane, comes when everyone does right by everyone else. Go ahead, Steve," he said pointing to the monitor with his eyes. "You don't need my angels' Shechinah. Everyone has My Presence inside. You just need to bring it out. Talk to Satan now." He winked at Steve and rose to His feet, guiding Steve to a standing position. "Make me proud of your bravery. I wish I could experience that, you lucky dog. Go ahead now. You can take it from here." He walked away and poofed into thin air.

Momentarily, Steve was terrified. "Wait, God! Please come back!" he shouted.

"Remember, Steve," a voice came from nowhere and everywhere, "I help those who help themselves. Stall the Devil for time. I'll do the rest."

Steve saw on the monitor that the Red Sox slugger had taken the pitcher to a full count. The fans were on their feet, creating a deafening din. Suddenly, Steve emerged from behind Leah, stood in front of her and pleaded with Satan. "Take me and leave these two. I'm the one who failed you, oh Prince of Darkness."

"Ha!" the Devil's roar shot back, "who do you think you are, Daniel Webster? You puny humans can fool me once in a while, but I'm no fool. Step aside, you insignificant ant, before I burn you to a crisp."

"No!" Leah shouted. She turned Steve around to face her. "Don't do this, Steve! I beg you!"

"It's all right," he whispered to her as he winked and pointed several times to the monitor with his eyes. "Trust me," he hissed, "I know what I'm doing."

The monitor showed the batter fouling off several balls. The crowd roared with each pitch, and then Steve spoke. "You gotta admit, Satan, for puny people we're putting up a valiant fight here, no? At least give us a concession, Satan."

"You want a beer, maybe?" Satan roared in jest.

"Ah, a sense of humor," Steve said. "There's hope for you yet, oh Prince."

Just then, Steve heard the loud crack of the bat. Pandemonium reigned supreme at the ballpark. The announcer on the monitor shouted wildly many times over, "A grand slam! The Red Sox win the World Series! The Curse is lifted!"

"No more stalling, maggots," the Devil snarled. "You're coming with me now. The bombs will fly soon after. What a great day!"

"I'm sorry, Bub, I don't mean to burst your bubble, you bobble head," Steve taunted.

"Says who?" the Devil roared back.

"Says you," Steve said. "The Red Sox won, you idiot. You can't touch us, and you can't drop any bombs on anyone either."

"Aaarrrg, I can't believe I was fooled by you maggots."

"You weren't fooled by us. God fooled you. If you think *we* could make the Red Sox win, you're colossally stupid. Only God could pull off a miracle like *that*. Let me give you a tip, you dummy: The next time you see George Burns, you might as well fold up your tent, put your ugly tail between your legs, hit the trail, and get out of Dodge."

The Devil responded with thunderous, ear-splitting wrath and disappeared instantly, bellowing as he went, "I'll come back for you, Leah!"

Leah said, "You were wonderful, Steve. I'm so proud of you." She came forward and gave him a warm embrace and a lingering, sensuous kiss. Just then, the waitress in white poofed onto the scene.

Jeez, Steve thought, *I must be getting used to this. I only jumped about a foot this time.* He grinned to himself, and then spoke. "Leah, I'd like you to meet Esther. Esther, this is Leah." The women gave each other a warm, knowing hug.

Then Esther warned, "I'm pretty sure we three could fend off the Devil in case he came back, but let's not tempt fate. Ready to be an angel, Leah?"

"Really?" she squealed in delight.

"Yes, really," Esther affirmed. "Hold onto my hand, and we'll be in Heaven in a jiffy."

"Thanks, you two," Steve poignantly said. All three hugged briefly, and showered each other's cheeks with kisses.

"Good-bye, my love," Leah said happily.

"Good-bye, Steve," Esther echoed. "Thank you for helping to save Leah. Nancy there is a wonderful woman. She'll make you happy. Be a good husband to her and work to make a heaven here on earth. We'll see you after that." They both disappeared in a flash.

Steve turned his attention to the reclining figure at his feet. Bending down, he called out, "Nancy, Nancy. Wake up, Nancy."

She began to stir and her eyes fluttered open. "Steve? Steve, is that you?" He helped her up to a sitting position. "What a dream!" she exclaimed. "I think you were there with the Devil, an angel, a little old man, and an incredibly gorgeous woman who dragged me from my seat."

"Doesn't seem too bad of a dream so long as I was in it," Steve quipped. "Did the dream tell you what happened to the Red Sox?"

"Yeah, they won. That's how I knew it was a dream," she grinned.

"Well, they actually won. Really. No kidding, Nancy. Five to four on a grand slam in the ninth. What a miracle!"

"No way! Wow! Let's go celebrate," she suggested enthusiastically.

"Sure, where'd you like to go?"

"Durgin Park. It's my favorite restaurant."

Steve wondered why that did not surprise him, and he laughed to himself. He helped Nancy to her feet and suggested they take the streetcar and return after dinner to retrieve their cars. She agreed with Steve that the prime rib, medium, with white horse radish, was divinely inspired.

They walked off holding hands, blushing self-consciously. They had plenty of time to get acquainted over the winter, and for love to flourish through eighty-one home games rooting together for their beloved Boston Red Sox, the World Champions of Major League Baseball.